I found the little gravel path that led to the drydocked boats and with relief, stepped onto solid ground. Ahead of me loomed the bulk of a trawler, yellow light showing through one of her portholes. The *Sea Queen,* I guessed. I navigated a course to the left of her, trying to be careful, trying to be quiet. But even stopping every few paces to look and listen, I still managed to fall over a cardboard box. As I lay on the ground, cursing, fumbling for my penlight, the moon sailed out of a ragged scrap of clouds, turning clumps of darkness to low-growing shrubs and showing me, dead ahead, the silver and black shape of an automobile. I swallowed and rolled to my knees, brushing gravel off my hands. Four paces took me over to the car and I knelt behind it, touching with one finger a sticky handprint on the trunk. I looked down at the license plate. As I had feared it would, it read ST CYR. Eliane's car. The car I had ridden in. With her. I laid my head against the cold metal, looking up at the moon, praying that this was a dream from which I would momentarily awaken. But of course, it wasn't.

I reached in my pocket for my lockpicks.

LAUREN WRIGHT DOUGLAS

GOBLIN MARKET

The Naiad Press, Inc.
1994

Printed in the United States of America on acid-free paper
First Edition
Second Printing, December 1994

Edited by Christine Cassidy
Cover design by Catherine Hopkins
Typeset by Sandi Stancil

Library of Congress Cataloging-in-Publication Data

Douglas, Lauren Wright, 1947–
Goblin market / by Lauren Wright Douglas.
p. cm.
"A Caitlin Reece mystery."
ISBN 1-56280-047-7 (pbk.)
1. Reece, Caitlin (Fictitious character)—Fiction. 2. Women detectives—United States—Fiction. 3. Lesbians—United States—Fiction. I. Title.
PS3554.08263G63 1993
813′.54—dc20 93-24910
CIP

For Martha

About the Author

Lauren Wright Douglas was born in Canada in 1947. She grew up in a military family and spent part of her childhood in Europe. Several years ago, Lauren moved from her home in the Pacific Northwest to the American Southwest where she now lives with her partner and an ever-changing number of cats. *Goblin Market* is her seventh book for Naiad Press, and the fifth in the Caitlin Reece mystery series. *Ninth Life,* the second Caitlin Reece mystery, won the 1990 Lambda Literary Award for Best Lesbian Mystery. At present, Lauren is at work on *A Rage of Maidens,* another Caitlin Reece novel, which will be published by Naiad in 1994.

BOOKS BY LAUREN WRIGHT DOUGLAS

The Always Anonymous Beast (A Caitlin Reece Mystery)	1987
Osten's Bay (by Zenobia N. Vole)	1988
Ninth Life (A Caitlin Reece Mystery)	1990
The Daughters of Artemis (A Caitlin Reece Mystery)	1991
A Tiger's Heart (A Caitlin Reece Mystery)	1992
Goblin Market (A Caitlin Reece Mystery)	1993
Rage of Maidens (A Caitlin Reece Mystery)	1994

For there is no friend like a sister
In calm or stormy weather;
To cheer one on the tedious way,
To fetch one if one goes astray,
To lift one if one totters down,
To strengthen while one stands.

— Christina Rosetti, "Goblin Market"

SUNDAY

Chapter 1

I sat with Liz McLaren on the rocks at Clover Point. Offshore, one heck of a March storm was building. Pursued by a flotilla of eggplant-colored clouds, a few lone sailboats ran before the weather, seeking the safe harbor of the marina just around the point. A stiff north wind whipped the waters of the bay to whitecaps, the gale's none-too-gentle fingers threatening to lift the hair from my head. I had long ago lost feeling in my nose and fingers and my toes were now giving up the ghost. Why in God's name must clients pick such bizarre places for interviews? What was wrong with, say, the reading room of the Empress, or the art gallery, or Madame Tussaud's Wax Museum? What misguided romanticism demands mortification of the body? Privacy could be had in oh so much warmer places.

Liz, never a friend of mine, nor I of hers, was having a hard time saying what she'd asked me here to tell me. And I was having an equally hard time paying attention. Her phone call had rousted me from my living room couch where I was treating a moderately well-developed virus with two warm cats, chicken soup, and an Elizabeth George novel. I was scratchy of throat, stuffy of head, and short of temper. Hardly the frame of mind in which to interview a prospective client. Only a debt to my old friend, back-door physician Maggie Kent, could have brought me here to this windy point on such a blustery day.

"I know you must think I'm overreacting," Liz said for about the third time, "but —"

"Stop trying to read my mind," I replied, interrupting what seemed to me a pointless description of her lover, Laura, who (I had just learned) was blonde, delicate, beautiful, a teacher, only recently "separated" (now there's a handy euphemism) from her husband and therefore extremely fragile, which is why she couldn't be here herself today. I snorted. No doubt the blustery breezes would have borne the fair lass away. "Just tell me. Please."

"Okay," tough, dykey Liz said, running a hand through hair so aggressively curly even a short cut couldn't subdue it. "Someone's been sending Laura things in the mail."

I sneezed. Oh God, I just wasn't up to playing Twenty Questions today. "What kind of things?"

"Well." Liz squirmed, fiddling with the zipper on her leather jacket. "Pictures."

"Pictures?" I prayed for forbearance. Or at least civility. Why in hell couldn't she come to the point? "What sort of pictures? Reproductions of Emily Carr's totem poles? Pictures of Morris the cat? Pinups from *Playgirl*? What?"

My testiness must have been evident because Liz bristled. "Photos."

"Ah, photos. Not pictures." At least we were getting somewhere. "Photos of?"

"Laura. Photos of Laura."

"Someone's been taking photos of her?"

Liz shook her head. "No. These are old photos. Laura as a teenager. That sort of thing. They were in her photo album."

"Were? What does that mean? Doesn't she have the album now?"

"Well, that's the problem. It was stolen from Laura's husband's place during a burglary. Or so he says."

I lifted an eyebrow. "But?"

"Huh?"

"There's an implied 'but' in your voice. Don't you believe him?"

"I don't know. I mean, who would bother stealing a photo album? If you ask me, the dickhead still has it and he's the one sending the pictures."

"Maybe," I agreed. "But maybe not, too. In any event what we have is the fact that someone's been sending Laura old photos of herself. Do the photos come with messages? Notes, letters, poems, things like that? And how long has this been going on?"

"Maybe two months. And no, there aren't any notes. Just the photos." Liz turned to look at me, brown eyes anxious. "But the photos . . . they're, well, they're just bits and pieces."

"Did you bring them?"

"Um, no. I guess I should have."

"I can see them later. Tell me about them."

She ran a hand through her hair again. "It's like whoever sent them blew some up and reduced others so everything — you know, all the body parts — would be the same size, then cut them up. They fit together like jigsaw puzzle pieces."

Body parts? Ye gods. "A jigsaw puzzle." I cleared my throat. "How many photos have you received?"

"Four."

"This may be a silly question, but how did Laura know the pictures were of her if they're bits and pieces?"

Liz picked up a handful of tiny beach stones and let them sift through her fingers. "The first piece he sent, the first photo, was Laura's college graduation picture." Her voice broke, betraying feelings she would never admit. "But just the, um, head, you know. Just the head."

Oh goody. This reeked of something I really didn't want to get involved with. Intimidation. Extortion. Someone's idea of a very sick joke. Or it could be something worse. "Have you talked to anyone at the police?"

"Are you kidding? What would I tell them? That some fruitcake was sending my lover weird pictures? I'm a dyke, Caitlin. How seriously do you think they'd take me?"

I sighed. She had a point. That, after all, was why I was in business — to help those the system couldn't. Or wouldn't. Sometimes, though, the combination of Liz McLarens, miserable March days, and burgeoning viruses made it hard to be enthusiastic about my *metier.* "Tell me what you want me to do."

She looked at me hopefully. "Then you don't think I'm overreacting?"

I shook my head. "I don't know. But just for the sake of argument, let's take this seriously. Why, who thinks you're overreacting? Laura?"

Liz looked away.

I persisted. "Why? Does she know something you don't?"

"Like what?" Liz demanded belligerently.

I held up both hands in mock surrender. "I don't know. Something that would make her think this is all, what, innocent? A game? Something she and hubby do for kicks?"

"It's not a game if that dickhead Theo is doing it! Laura ought to know that better than me," she added ominously.

Oh fine. Dissension in the nest already. I think it's a truism that the presence of husbands makes the course of sapphic love a very rocky one indeed. "Theo is, I take it, the husband."

With a savage motion, Liz hurled the rest of the stones she'd been holding out into the bay. "Yes. Theo fucking Blalock is the husband." She brushed her hands off on her denim-clad thighs. “What I want you to do is to make Theo — goddammit, I know it’s him — stop all this.”

“Have you tried?”

“Yeah, I did. Once. We yelled at each other on the phone.”

“What did he say?”

“That he doesn’t have the album anymore and that even if he did he wouldn’t be doing such weird shit. But —”

“I know. You know it’s him.”

“Well, who the hell else could it be? Laura doesn’t even *know* any other men.”

I wisely kept my own counsel.

“Well?” Liz prodded.

“Sometimes I can be helpful in cases that the system won’t touch,” I told her tentatively. “But I need to know more about this. That means I need to talk to both of you.”

“But Laura —”

“Laura, shmaura. Both of you.”

“Why do you need to drag Laura into it? I’m the one you’ll be working for —”

“Both of you or no deal.”

Liz jumped to her feet. “Forget it, then. I came here today not because I wanted to but because Maggie Kent said you’d help.” I groaned. Thank you very much, Mags. “Oh, you’ll help all right, but it has to be on your terms. Right?” Liz shook her head angrily. “No, thanks. I can handle this myself.”

“For Christ’s sake, don’t be so unreasonable,” I snapped. Not wanting to be loomed over I, too, jumped to my feet. "What's the matter with you. What is it? Why don't you want me talking to Laura?"

The stricken look Liz gave me told it all.

"Jesus H. Christ!" I yelled, comprehension dawning. "You haven't *told her*! She doesn't know a thing about these photos!"

Liz balled her hands into fists.

"You're protecting her, aren't you? Sir Liz. What a joke."

She swung at me but rage made her sloppy. I dodged easily under the blow, grabbing her wrist and hanging on.

"Save your anger for an appropriate subject, kid. The perp, for instance. This isn't a game — you against him in some macho duel. Someone put a lot of time and thought into this. It may well be sicker and far more dangerous than you realize."

She struggled, but I held on, deriving some perverse, Neanderthal satisfaction from the fact that I was bigger and stronger than she. We were toe to toe and I could see tears gathering in her eyes.

"I'm willing to help you," I said gently, "but you'll have to trust me. You'll have to play it my way."

"I . . . can't," Liz said through clenched teeth.

I backed off and let her go.

Her eyes were closed now and tears ran down her freckled cheeks. She seemed neither to know nor care. "Just go and see Theo. Make him stop."

"Liz, listen to me," I said carefully.

But Liz wasn't in a mood to listen. Scrubbing her face with the back of one hand, she jammed her fists into the pockets of her jacket. “I shouldn’t have listened to Maggie. I can handle this myself,” she said bitterly.

I laughed. “Yes, you probably can. And Laura can send you cigarettes and tins of cashews and bars of lilac-scented soap while you’re doing fifteen to life in the pen. If she remembers you at all. Is that what you want?”

“We’ll see about that,” Liz said, white-lipped. She backed away from me and I let her go. She scrambled across the rocks and up the bank, making for her car. Then, as if she’d forgotten something, she turned back to me. She looked like a tousle-haired kid of about ten, hands in the pockets of her jacket, collar up against the weather. The wind swept some of what she said away from me, but I heard enough. I heard what she wanted me to.

“. . . and if I have to kill him to keep him away from her, I will.”

Chapter 2

Outside my kitchen window, in the tag-end of the afternoon, the rain sluiced down the glass like separate streams of tears. With an effort, I pulled the curtains closed. Snap out of it, I told myself. She'll be all right. You can't be den mother to the world.

"Myap?" my fat gray cat Repo asked, twining around my ankles.

"It's nothing," I told him, bending to scratch his ears. "I'm a Sagittarian and therefore overly given to brooding. Besides, I have a cold. I'm entitled."

But Repo was right. I had responsibilities, obligations, right here. Under my feet, even. I looked over to the corner of the kitchen where the rest of my furry family was lined up, waiting for dinner. Blind, striped Jeoffrey had once again found his way unerringly to his food dish, and there he sat, beautiful eyes fixed on nothing. Or perhaps, as my young friend Jory insisted, on a better, more interesting interior world. Farseer Goldeneyes, she called him. Maybe she was right.

Beside Jeoffrey sat Pansy, a diminutive white cat with one apricot ear, an apricot tail, and an attitude. Her pale, pale green eyes were half-closed, as though in inner enjoyment of future mischief. She was the bane of Repo's existence, acknowledged mistress of the stare-down, queen of kitty fisticuffs.

"Cool it," I told Pansy, as I opened a can of Friskies Beef and Liver. I spooned the food into three separate dishes and plunked them down on the plastic mat I had optimistically placed on my hardwood floor, thinking it might contain the cat food mess. Fat chance. My three Messy Mouths dragged the food out of their dishes and onto the floor anyhow. The Cat Mat was just a minor inconvenience. I fed Repo on Jeoffrey's left and Pansy on his right but this was never satisfactory to Pansy. She always had to initiate the Great Food Bowl Do-Si-Do. Having taken one bite of her food, she decided it was unsatisfactory and that Repo's must be much better. With a growl, she approached Repo, bit him on the hind leg, and sat waiting expectantly. Without an instant's hesitation, Repo abandoned his dish and hustled himself over to hers. "Everybody happy?" I inquired once they'd settled down in their new positions. I gave Repo a reassuring pat.

"Yang," he murmured sadly, busy with Pansy's rejected bowl of Beef and Liver.

"I don't know," I told him. "There's no accounting for women's behavior. It's just something you'll have to learn to live with. Try not to take it personally."

The telephone interrupted my having to play Dear Abby to the cats.

"Why on earth are you still at home?" a voice demanded.

Oh, Jesus. Tonia. Was it dinner time already? How long had I stood at the kitchen window, brooding about Liz? Tonia was due to fly off to Boston tomorrow for a conference and we'd arranged to have dinner together tonight. Evidently I'd been looking forward to it immensely because it had completely slipped my mind. Great. Just great. "I'm on my way," I said, forcing cheer into my voice.

She must have read between the lines, because she asked, "Hey, are you all right?"

"Sure," I assured her breezily. "Never better. Want me to pick anything up?"

"No, nothing. Just come on."

"Righto."

I hung up, gave the cats a few more pats apiece, then hurried into the bathroom. I splashed my face, ran a brush through my hair, swallowed a couple of aspirins, and thought longingly of my bed. What had happened to the afternoon? In the bedroom, I threw off my soft, too-small gray T-shirt and comfy old red sweatshirt with holes in the elbows and struggled into a dark green turtleneck, a green wool pullover, and a clean pair of jeans. I could do better than my old Adidas, too, I figured. Pulling on a pair of dark green socks, I found my Topsiders and decided I was ready. Then I stood up and almost passed out. Feeling weak, I sat down on the edge of my bed, realizing that I ought to phone Tonia, wrap myself in my quilt, and call it a day.

Instead, I zipped my bomber jacket up to my chin, leaped the puddles in my driveway like a maladroit gazelle, and drove down Oak Bay Avenue to Tonia's house.

"Are you sitting in there brooding?" Tonia called from the kitchen as I stacked logs for a fire. I'd told her bits and pieces of my afternoon meeting with Liz and, whereas she'd listened and asked appropriate questions, she had neither agreed nor disagreed with my decision. For that matter, I wasn't entirely certain that I agreed with my decision.

"Brooding? Fat chance. You've kept me too busy," I said, standing up and brushing off my hands.

"Good. Now, c'mon in here and open this jar for me, will you? And then you could feed Fogarty."

"Hmmmf. Your plot is pretty thin, woman. Transparent even."

"Just work," Tonia told me. "Those who work can't brood." Tonia knew me very well, I realized. Well enough to try to keep me from brooding — an unprofitable pastime if ever there was one, but one to which my Celtic genes predisposed me. What was it the poet said: "God must have loved the Celts / Because he made them mad: / All their wars are happy; / And all their songs are sad." Well, tonight was no time for brooding. We had a mini-celebration planned and if it killed me, I was going to be festive.

"Hey, Foges," I called Fogarty, Tonia's black Labrador retriever to the mud room where he ate. As I spooned his food into his dish, I petted him and whispered, "What was it Art Garfunkel said: 'Who would notice a gem in a five and dime store?' Do you think Tonia is the kind of person who'd notice? I've been worrying about that lately."

"Ruff," he opined, bending to inhale his supper.

"Right," I told him, sitting back on my heels. "That's my opinion, too. I've committed before, Foges old fella, and I'm not eager to try it again. I'm not really very good at . . . sharing myself. Revelations. Unburdening. You know, all that mutual stuff."

"Mmfff," he agreed.

"I'm a private kinda person," I told him. "This intimacy, I'm not sure it's for me."

"What on earth are you muttering about in there?" Tonia asked, poking her head around the door.

"Just asking Fogarty his opinion on whether the universe is contracting or expanding," I told her, standing up. "And, for that matter, whether you'd notice a gem in a five and dime store."

"Whether I'd what? Have you been taking Actifed again? You know you're allergic to it." She raised an eyebrow. Tonight, dressed in slate gray cords and an indigo wool turtleneck, she looked like a million dollars. Shiny dark hair cut off just below her ears, smoky blue eyes, Katharine Hepburn cheekbones. Beautiful Tonia, what had I ever done to deserve her? And why couldn't I summon up any enthusiasm for us living together — the current topic of controversy in our on-again off-again relationship?

"No ma'am," I answered cheerfully.

"Hmmm," she said, casting a final appraising glance at me, but returning to the kitchen.

"Ha! We fooled her, didn't we?" I asked as I opened the back door and let Fogarty outside. He loped off to fertilize Tonia's daffodil bed and I leaned against the doorframe, feeling mean. All this busy work hadn't kept me from thought after all. And the more I thought, the more convinced I became that I'd been too hasty in telling Liz I wouldn't help her. Whoever was sending the photos sounded like a nut case, someone Liz probably couldn't handle on her own. "Shit," I said aloud. "I'm tired of thinking about this."

"You're just feeling crabby because you have a cold," Tonia said, opening the door to come and stand beside me.

"No, I'm just feeling crabby because I've become a crabby person. I've gotten middle-aged and testy. A couple of years ago I would have jumped at a case like this. I would have figured I could do *something*."

"And you probably would have figured that you *had* to do something, too."

"Yeah, I suppose so. Let's go in. We'll have pneumonia." I let Tonia precede me through the door then closed it firmly behind me.

"You don't *have* to do anything," Tonia said, turning to face me in the narrow hall. "Chances are, they can manage without you."

"Maybe," I equivocated.

"You don't sound as though you believe that."

"I'm trying to," I told her honestly. "I'm trying

not to be arrogant about this fixit business I seem to be in. Of course people can manage without me. But . . ."

"But Liz came and asked for your assistance, right? And you feel, what, compelled to help her?"

"No, not that."

"Then what? Caitlin, what's really bothering you?" Tonia came to stand in front of me, arms crossed.

"What's really bothering me is that I might have said no for the wrong reason."

"Oh?"

"Yeah. This scenario — Formerly Straight Woman Runs to the Arms of Local Dyke, Leaving Pissed-Off Hubby in the Wings — is the stuff of soap operas. For the dyke, it's a short road to a heartache."

"Do you mean to say that you think Laura's going to go back to him?"

I leaned against the wall. "Lots of Lauras do."

"Poor Liz."

"Yeah. Poor Liz. And I think she hasn't told Laura about the photos because the fewer times his name is mentioned, the fewer opportunities there will be for contact. Liz seems scared to death of something and I'm willing to bet that she's feeling a little inadequate to the competition."

"But you could be wrong, and that's what's eating at you. Right?"

"Right. Hell, she could have kept the photos from Laura for lots of other reasons."

"True," Tonia said. Then after a moment, "Name one."

I sighed. "I can't. Jesus, I hate these male-female things."

Tonia put her warm hands on my right arm,

broken and only recently healed from my own intervention in a male-female duel that had very nearly cost me my life.

"I hate them with all my heart," I told her. "They're minefields."

She took a step forward and put her arms around me. For a moment, she just held me. Then she stepped back. I felt my lips twist in a rueful smile. What was it Neil Young said? "You give more than I can take; I only harvest some." I wondered if Tonia realized this. Or if she did, if it mattered to her.

"What do you want to do, Caitlin?"

"I'm not sure. Something, though."

"You think you were wrong, that you should have gotten involved."

"Maybe. Whether the three of them are playing little theater or not doesn't change the fact of the photos. The best case is that the photos may be a prelude to attempted extortion. Soften them up by scaring them to death. Then offer to quit if they pay you."

Tonia shivered. "And the worst case?"

"That the photos are a prelude to violence. Like an operatic tenor singing scales. I'm not sure, though. This particular kind of craziness isn't my field of expertise."

"You say these things so matter-of-factly," Tonia said bleakly.

"Yeah, I guess I do." I put my hands in my pockets and leaned against the doorframe. "Ah hell. Maybe I'll just go have a chat with Mr. Blalock. Tomorrow. I can always call Liz and tell her I've changed my mind."

"Good," Tonia said, putting a hand on my shoulder. "That sounds reasonable."

Reasonable. Yeah, that was me all right. Reasonable Caitlin Reece. I took her hand from my shoulder, turned it palm up and kissed it. Then I folded her fingers over her palm and held her hand between both of mine. "When I was little, my grandmother always did that to me," I told her. "She said it was so the kiss wouldn't get away. I spent years peeking between my fingers trying to see what a kiss looked like. And when I opened my hand, of course it wasn't there."

"If I hadn't already been seduced by you, I'd say you were trying to seduce me, Ms. Reece," Tonia said. "All this talk of kissing and such. It's enough to turn a girl's head."

"Good," I told her. "Hold that thought until after supper. If you want to risk getting my virus, I could share with you a few other oscular delights — ones that Grandma most definitely didn't show me."

"You're on," she said, eyes sparkling. "If you set the table and pour the wine, I'll fetch the cioppino and the French bread. Oh, and call Fogarty in, will you?"

Humming, I went to the back door to call Fogarty but he was waiting on the step, smelling doggy and wet. "Shake," I told him in the mud room, and he dutifully sprayed me with water. "Good boy." I took a towel from the pegboard where Tonia kept coats and jackets and toweled Fogarty down. He stood there patiently, submitting to all this. "Very good boy," I told him. Even though I'm a cat person, I have a certain affection for Fogarty. He's a reserved and gracious dog who knows the limits of good taste. No licking and writhing for him. I gave him a hug, put the towel on its peg and went to the kitchen sink to wash my hands. The phone interrupted my ablutions.

"It's for you," Tonia called.

"Yes?" I asked, picking up the receiver, impatient to get on with the evening's festivities.

"Caitlin, I'm glad to have caught you."

"Maggie? What's up?"

"What's up is Laura and Liz. They're here. At least Liz is. Laura was, but she left. They're both hysterical and I have to admit I'm not far from it."

"Let me guess. Laura just found out what Liz was keeping from her."

"Right."

"And Liz, realizing how wrong she was, wants you to try and persuade me to reconsider taking the case. Which now includes finding Laura and bringing her back home."

"Right again."

Ah shit. I sat down in the easy chair by the phone and looked wistfully at the cozy fire I'd just built. Fogarty sighed heavily on the hearth, dreaming doggie dreams. From the kitchen came the odor of garlic bread. "Okay," I said, thinking of the half-dozen favors I owed Maggie. "But I'm doing this for you, not for her. Or them."

"I understand," Maggie said. "I'll put the coffee on. I'm afraid this may be a long night."

I hung up the phone and went on into the kitchen to break the bad news to Tonia. "Sorry," I told her. "I have to go."

She turned from the sink to face me, exasperation plain on her features. "Oh, Caitlin, for heaven's sake. First I have to practically drag you over here — it was perfectly obvious you'd forgotten — and now you're just going to leave? Dammit, Caitlin!"

I held up my hands. "Don't," I said, stung by her anger. "Some things just have to be done. I'm in Maggie Kent's debt. She's helped me out of a jam more than once. Hell, if she were a licensed physician she'd have had to report every gunshot wound and knife slash to the cops. I'd probably be out of business. So I owe her, see?" And I was stung, too, that I had to explain how I conducted my business. "Saying no is not an option."

Tonia leaned against the sink and tapped one foot impatiently. My heart gave a lurch of dismay. "This is what life with me would be like," I told her matter-of-factly. "The best-laid plans and all that."

"I can see that," she replied shortly. "Well, you'd better go then."

"I guess so," I said, heading for the front hall. There was, it seemed, nothing more to be said.

"Caitlin," Tonia called as I opened the door.

"Yeah?"

"WIll you be back tonight?"

I hesitated. "It might be late."

"You do have a key, you know."

An imp of perversity took command of my tongue, preventing me from saying what needed to be said. "Maybe not tonight. I'll see you when you get back," I heard myself say coolly when what I dearly wanted to say was just the opposite. I hate this about myself. But I was still smarting under Tonia's criticism and I was damned if I was going to take any more barbs. *Fool,* I told myself as I closed the door behind me. *Fool.* I heard no voice raised in disagreement.

Chapter 3

Maggie's house on Winchester Street was a small brick bungalow set well back from the street behind a waist-high holly hedge. I recognized her ancient blue El Dorado parked out front and pulled my MG in behind it. Through a break in the hedge I hurried up the flagstone walk, vowing to conceal how pissed off about this whole thing I was.

Maggie met me at the front door — a tall, sturdy woman in her fifties, short silver hair, startling blue eyes, neat tan cords and a fisherman-knit pullover.

“You look in a terrific mood,” she said, giving me the once-over. “What’s up?”

“Nothing terminal,” I told her. “Domestic bliss isn’t all it’s cracked up to be, that’s all. So where’s the errant lover?”

“Downstairs in the TV room, pacing.”

“Any word from Laura?”

“Nope.”

“Well, let’s get on with this,” I said. “Coming?”

“Mmmm, maybe not. I thought I’d just make coffee and wait for you to calm her down.”

“Coward.” I tossed her my bomber jacket. “Okay. I’ll bring her upstairs once I’ve wrestled her into submission.” Brave words, I thought as I descended the stairs. Wrestling Liz into submission wasn’t something I had any enthusiasm for. Still, a promise was a promise. And for Maggie, I’d do anything. The majority of the licks I’d taken from bad guys had been attended to by Maggie. A back-door physician now, she lost her license for performing an abortion on a fourteen-year-old who’d been raped by her stepfather. But I didn’t feel sorry for her. She’d made her choice. We all do. Even Liz.

“You’re a mess,” I told her as I walked into the TV room. And indeed she was. Hair disheveled, eyes red and puffy, she looked as though she’d been on a three-day binge.

“She’s gone!” Liz wailed.

“Yeah, thanks to you, she is,” I said, deciding that the brutal approach would work best with our Liz.

“You *shithead,*” she yelled. “What would you know about it anyhow?”

"Quite a lot, actually," I said, perching on the arm of the sofa.

That took the wind out of her sails. "You do? I bet."

"Mmmhmm. I had the singular lack of judgment to fall for a straight woman when I was just a kid. I would have done anything to hang onto her, to keep her away from *him.* So don't tell me I don't know anything about this."

She threw herself down in an armchair and began to gnaw a hangnail. "Why are you here?" she asked after a moment of chewing.

"Maggie called me."

"Right."

Jesus, Liz, don't make this easy, I thought. "She asked me to come and talk to you and maybe reconsider my decision. Maybe you do need my help after all."

She was silent for a moment. Then: "Hell, yes, we need your help," she said wearily. "I screwed things pretty badly, didn't I? Shit. You were right — Sir Liz. It is a joke."

"Don't blame yourself too much," I said. "Things are probably fixable."

"If you can find Laura," she said, raising her eyes to mine.

"Oh, I think I can find her. With your help."

Silence.

"Any ideas where she might have gone? You did check the house, didn't you? Maybe she's there."

She shook her head. "She's not. I checked." She screwed her eyes closed. "She might have gone to her mother's place. Although she *does* live way out in Sooke. Wait — she's got a friend in town. Alana somebody-or-other. They teach at the same school. That arts magnet thing in Oak Bay. She came over once or twice to have dinner with us."

I sighed. "Does Alana have a last name? Or a phone number."

"I don't know. But I do know where she lives," she said, brightening. "You know those new apartments down behind the harbor? She's renting the end one. Right by the water. If she's there her Miata will be in the driveway. Laura drives a white Toyota Camry. That should be there, too."

"Okay," I said, standing up.

"So you'll do it? You'll take the case?"

I sighed. "Let's get Laura back here and have a talk," I said. "I want to be sure we're all clear about who's doing what."

"Okay," she said miserably.

"By the way," I asked, "why did Laura run off?"

Liz studied her shoes. "She found out about the photos."

I resisted saying, "I told you so." No need to rub salt in the wound. "Oh? How?"

"I'd just put them in my truck. She went out there to get something and . . . found them. She brought them inside, started asking me questions, and freaked out. I couldn't calm her down. Then she grabbed her car keys and took off."

I raised an eyebrow. "Pretty extreme reaction, don't you think?"

Liz shrugged. "She's like that. Sensitive. I guess the photos scared her."

Uh huh. "Go on upstairs and apologize for

scaring Maggie half to death. Make cookies or something. I'll be back."

The apartments Liz had described to me were actually a row of very posh townhouses whose back yards were the harbor. Several of them had their own docks, and here and there the masts of sailboats pointed heavenward, bare and forlorn. Alana's Miata was parked in the driveway and, as luck would have it, so was Laura's Camry. Bingo. Feeling absurdly like an actor who'd forgotten her lines, I parked my MG, walked to the door and knocked. A tall, thin brunette in jeans and a pale blue sweatshirt that said FUCK HOUSEWORK opened the door and regarded me suspiciously. I proferred one of my cards. She examined it and said, "So?"

I groaned. Another tough cookie. "I'd like to speak to Laura Neal," I said pleasantly.

"Tell her to go away," a voice called from within.

Alana shrugged and looked at me dismissingly. "You heard the lady. Go away."

"Okay," I agreed, taking a step backward. "Oh, one thing, though."

"Yeah?" Alana said, the door now half-closed.

"Did she tell you she has a deranged weirdo after her?"

The door opened to three-quarters. "What?"

"And if *I* could find her here, how hard do you think it will be for him to do the same?" I checked my watch. "I'd bet he'll be along anytime now."

Alana looked over my shoulder out into the night, then behind her into the lighted apartment.

"Keep the doors locked," I said sternly. "And the phone close at hand." I feigned alarm. "Hey, speaking of the phone, where's the utilities box?"

Her eyes grew wide.

"Omigosh, your phone line isn't *outside,* is it?"

"I don't know!" she wailed, throwing the door wide. "Laura!" she called into the depths of the apartment. "You'll just have to come and talk to this person. Come in," she said, hauling me into the apartment by my sleeve.

"Alana, no!" a voice called from the dining room.

I walked in the direction of the voice. "Ms. Neal, I presume?"

"Yes, dammit. Who are you? Did Liz send you?"

I leaned against the wall, crossed my arms, and looked at the object of Liz's affection. Yes indeedy, she was blonde, blue-eyed, and fragile-looking. Hardly the type to make my blood boil, but *chacun à son goût,* as they say. In fact, her hair was so palely blonde, her eyes so palely blue, and her complexion so palely white that she seemed almost . . . ethereal. The pale pink wool turtleneck sweater she wore did nothing to dispel her aura of bloodlessness, of helplessness, of childishness, and I wondered if this was an effect she sought to cultivate. Her silky hair was shoulder-length, parted in the middle, and fell straight, giving her face an Alice-in-Wonderland look that I found ludicrous. No female over the age of nine ought to look like this. Doing so said: "Here I am, poor helpless girl-child. Do what you will with me." Shit.

"Yeah, Liz sent me. She's worried about you."

“Go away. I’m perfectly fine here.” She blew her nose delicately into a tissue.

“For the time being. But what about Alana? Aren’t you concerned about her?”

Laura closed her eyes and twisted her tissue.

“C’mon, Laura. Let’s go. We all have to work together — you, Liz and me — to figure out who’s doing this and how to stop him. Hiding here at Alana’s isn’t the answer. You know that, don’t you?”

She snuffled into her tissue again. “Yes.”

I looked over to where Alana stood, hands in her jeans pockets, wide-eyed, anxious. “Get her coat, will you?” She nodded and scurried off.

“Are you all right to drive?” I asked Laura.

She nodded feebly. Alana brought her a rose-colored down parka and she struggled into it.

“Just follow me,” I told her as we walked to the door. “If you get lost, wait for me at the corner of James Bay and Foul Bay roads. I’ll come back for you.”

I nodded to Alana and hustled Laura out into the night.

“And you have absolutely no idea who might be doing this?” I asked Laura as the four of us sat around Maggie’s pine kitchen table eating chocolate chip cookies and drinking coffee.

Liz, who had drawn her chair up so she could sit close to Laura, anxiously rubbed her lover’s arm. “Honey? Don’t you think it’s Theo?”

Laura laughed, then realizing this might be an inappropriate response, immediately subsided. Liz looked at her in alarm. "Believe me, Theo would never do anything like this," she told Liz. She was silent for a moment, clearly struggling to compose herself. Then, looking at me, she asked, "Can you find out who's doing this?"

"Probably."

"Oh? How?"

I raised an eyebrow. "I ask questions. I dig around." I shrugged. "One thing leads to another. Eventually something works."

"You charge a lot, I suppose."

"Two hundred and fifty dollars a day," I told her. "I need five hundred as a retainer to get started."

"Expensive," she observed, more to herself than to me. "And no guarantee of results. Do you *really* think you can find out who's doing this, and why, and make them stop?" Laura asked me.

I looked at her levelly. "I think I've already answered that. Yes. I think so."

Laura looked up from an examination of her fingernails. "I hate to be tedious, but I want to get something straight. What will you do when you find whoever's doing this? How exactly will you make him stop?"

"It depends on what he's doing. If he's broken the law, I'll hand him over to the cops."

"And if he hasn't?"

I shrugged. "Sometimes these guys can be . . . persuaded to go away."

"How?" she insisted. I was surprised at the desperation in her eyes.

"Trade secrets," I said. "I never reveal them."

She looked down at the tabletop again. "What I

mean is, how can you, a woman, make some *man* who's probably bigger and stronger than you, do, well, do what you want?"

Liz looked as though she wanted to crawl away somewhere.

I laughed out loud. "Trust me, I can. I don't have to arm wrestle them *every* time."

"No, I'm serious. Tell me."

I looked at her in exasperation. "There are only three ways: persuasion, intimidation, or dirty old brute force."

I expected her to shudder. Instead, she looked . . . encouraged.

"I try to stick to the first two," I told her.

"And if they don't work?"

"There's always number three."

"I see. You seem rather . . . confident in your abilities to get results."

I nodded. "I have a pretty good success ratio."

"Oh? What is it?"

"So far, one hundred percent."

A tear slid down one of Laura's cheeks and Liz made a wounded sound. Apart from that, though, no one spoke.

"Honey, let's let Caitlin do it," Liz said softly after a moment. "There's got to be a reason behind all this. If it's not Theo trying to scare you back to him —"

"It's not!" Laura insisted.

Liz looked over at me helplessly.

I decided to help this thing along. "What's your net worth, you two?" I asked.

"What?" Laura asked.

"Your net worth. What is it?"

"I . . . I have some cash in the bank. And my car. That's all."

I waited.

"My car's worth about twelve thousand dollars. I have about two thousand in cash."

I turned to Liz. "How about you?"

"Me? Oh, well, I have my truck, my tools, my house, my greenhouse, my car, a savings account, let's see, a couple of CDs . . ."

"Sounds like about a quarter million to me," I said.

Liz looked at me in surprise. "Yeah. I guess so."

"What are you getting at?" Laura asked, pale blue eyes open very wide. "That this might be about . . . money?"

"I'm not getting at anything," I said innocently. "Not yet. Just gathering facts."

An unreadable expression crossed Laura's face and as I held her gaze I realized that some turning point, some watershed had been reached. After a long moment, she turned to Liz. "All right. Yes. We'll hire Caitlin. Will you write her a check?"

"Sure," Liz said, jumping up from the table. "My checkbook's in my jacket. I'll just go get it."

I sat back, crossed my arms, and looked at her. She tucked a strand of hair behind one ear and gave me one panicky, terrified glance. What's going on here, I wondered.

"Here we go," Liz said enthusiastically, handing me a check. "Can you get started tomorrow?"

I took the check from her and put it on the

table. "Yes. But I need one more thing," I said, waiting until Laura looked up at me.

"Oh, what?" Liz asked.

"Cooperation. Honesty. From both of you. No lies, no evasions. When I ask for information, I want all of it. No editing, no censoring."

"Sure," Liz said.

Laura tried to smile. "All right."

Liar, I thought. *Already it begins.*

"I have a source who works only at night. I'd like to put him to work. So if you'll excuse me . . ."

"All right," Laura whispered.

I pocketed the check.

"There are some things I want from you," I told her. "Maggie, will you get some paper and a pen?"

"Does it have to be now?" Laura asked wearily.

"Yeah, it has to be now. And there'll be more tomorrow. I'll want pictures, a list of Theo's hangouts, names of buddies, hobbies — that sort of thing. Are you going to work or will you be at home?"

"I think I'll take the day off," she said softly.

"Good. I'll be there around nine," I told her.

She winced.

"In the meantime, I want you to write down your husband's full, legal name, date of birth, last known address, car license number, social insurance number, last employer, and any other facts you can supply."

"But I *told* you —"

Liz rolled her eyes.

"I know what you told me," I interrupted, raising my voice. "There's no way it could be Theo. But the only way to be certain is to do a little footwork and clear him. You know — rule him out."

Tight-lipped, she said, "I guess that makes sense."

Maggie brought me a yellow lined tablet and a pen. I pushed them across the table to Laura. "Write."

Chapter 4

"Francis," I said, settling down at my kitchen table and dialing a number you will never find in any directory. Francis the Ferret, nocturnal electronics genius, answered on the second ring.

"Caitlin! Why, we haven't heard from you in six months," he pouted. "We thought you'd met with misadventure. Or fallen in love."

"Same thing," I informed him. "But no such luck. I'm still around."

"Mmmm," he said ambiguously.

"Got a pencil?"

"Pencil? How antediluvian. Just speak, dearie. Your desires will be immortalized in my computer's memory. It's a little electronic advance I've pioneered. Lets me make sense of my clients' incoherent babblings. Go ahead — we're all ears."

Wondering fleetingly if *we* was he and his computer I gave him what I needed, based on the sketchy information Laura had told me: Theo Blalock, DOB 12/25/71, last known address 17-A Arbutus, drove an '89 Cherokee, black, license BBC 405; last known place of employment Pan Pacific Cannery, social insurance number 505 090 200.

"I want to know where he lives and works now. I want to know where he's used his credit cards and lists of stuff he's bought with them — books, photographic equipment — that sort of thing in particular. I want to know, too, if he has a record. If he does, I'd like to see his sheet, and I'd like names of people I can talk to — parole officers, social workers, psychiatrists. And their reports, if they're on database."

"Psychiatrists?" Francis warbled. "You mean our boy is deranged?"

"Not necessarily," I interrupted. "It's just a gut feeling I have."

"Sounds fascinating," Francis said. "And I can, as it happens, get right on it. As soon as you make a visit to my mail drop."

I groaned. "C'mon Francis, give me a break. After all these years you won't twiddle one dial for me on trust? Make one phone call? It's bloody inconvenient for me to drive all the way over to your mail drop at this hour of the night. I want to go to bed. Hell, most normal people are *in bed.*"

"In bed? What, at night? Why, nighttime is ever so much more interesting than daytime, you know. Have you ever thought about it? Why —"

"No paeans," I said testily. "I'll bring the money. Is the address the same — that all-night market on Cedar Hill Cross?"

"That's it," he said cheerily. "Boris will call me as soon as you've left the cash. Five hundred, in case you've forgotten."

"Trusting, aren't you?" I groused.

"The road to financial ruin is paved with trust," he said sorrowfully. "I'm only providing for my retirement, storing acorns against the winter of my old age, as it were." He sniffed. "You ought to be doing the same, my sweet."

"Yeah, yeah," I said as I hung up. Good old Francis. The milk of human kindness was a stranger to his veins — in fact, I fancied he possessed circuitry where most normal people have a circulatory system. Yet he was absolutely reliable, scrupulously honest, and endlessly creative. His only drawback was that he was weird beyond words. Oh yes, and very firm about money. Still, as Francis said, he was providing for his old age. I imagined there were very few group pension plans available for electronic snoops.

An hour later, at the Cedar Hill Mini-Mart, I handed over five crisp hundreds to the care of Francis's aged associate Boris, a stooped, cadaverous fellow who bore an unsettling resemblance to the older Count Dracula in Francis Ford Coppola's film. Boris accepted the envelope without a flicker of interest, transferred it to some recess under the counter, and returned to his perusal of a very flimsy foreign-language newspaper in Cyrillic script. No doubt a tabloid for expatriate Transylvanians. Feeling nervous about turning my back on the gaunt and rheumy Boris, I edged to the door, dawdling, wondering how it would look if I just bolted. The problem was solved for me by the arrival of a trio of bikers, all heavy black boots, greasy hair, and loud jocularity. I left them to Boris's tender ministrations and scuttled away to my car, feeling distinctly foolish. Comes from having seen too many horror movies and having too active an imagination. I felt much the same trepidation about Boris as I did after seeing *Alien* when I neurotically checked the knee space under my desk for days. Brrr. I made a mental note to deliver Francis's blood money in the daytime hereafter. When Boris had folded himself into his coffin. It was now close to midnight, and I had to do something to combat the caffeine in my system and staunch the adrenalin rush that the beginning of a case always gave me. Deep breathing, or meditation, or Tai Chi would probably have worked better, but I had come to rely on a dram of Scotch, a cup of my friend Yvonne's "Sleepytime Brew," and the soporific effects of a couple of snoring cats.

Back at home, I turned the heat on under the kettle, splashed a finger of Scotch into a tumbler, checked the bedroom to make sure the felines were in position, and shed my street clothes for my comfy old sweats. I made tea, then took a yellow lined tablet back to the bedroom with me where I burrowed under my quilt with a sigh. Repo roused from his slumbers, stretched, then lurched across the bed to curl up against me. He chirped to Jeoffrey to join him and the two settled down in a gray and tabby ball, moaning in feline contentment. Stroking their silken pelts, I sighed, feeling my heartbeat drop by about 25 points. As I finished the last of Yvonne's tea, I felt my eyelids beginning to close and with a grateful groan, snapped off the light and pulled the quilt up over my shoulders. My last thought, before I gave myself over to sleep, was of Tonia. I felt my stomach — ever the barometer of my feelings — clench in dismay and realized I was surprised, but not too surprised. All had not been well between us lately, not the least of which was that she didn't, well, dammit, she just didn't make my pulse race any more. *Fickle wench,* an interior voice accused. *Inconstant lover.* I decided I was much too tired to debate the point and resolved, like Scarlett O'Hara, to think about it tomorrow. Yawning, I waded into the warm, dark sea of sleep.

MONDAY

Chapter 5

When my alarm rang next morning, far too early, I thought, I rolled out of bed before I could change my mind. In the shower, I tried to think rationally about last night's spasm of disaffection for Tonia and decided that maybe my biorhythms were off. Or perhaps it was PMS. Or just plain old Caitlin Reece perversity. Don't be a jerk, I told myself. Tonia is a warm, wonderful, caring, sexy, gorgeous person who cares deeply about you. *Oh really,* a sly, interior voice said. Then why did she give you such grief when you had to go off to Maggie's, hmmmm? If you'd been a cardiac surgeon called out in the middle of the night, would that have been all right? Could it be that (horrors) she thinks that Sunday supper together is more important than your work? Or (worse yet) that she thinks she knows what's best for you and wants to change you — save you from yourself? Shit. I turned the water up to high and resolved to put the whole thing out of my mind. I had work to do — find whoever was harassing Laura and make him stop. I'd already started the wheels in motion. Francis was on the job. But there was work for me, too. And I had to have my head clear to do it.

I stepped out of the shower, wrapped myself in a towel, wiped the mirror free of moisture, and took a long hard look at myself. Seven years at the Crown Prosecutor's office and a handful more in my own business had contributed to a face full of character, I decided. Who needed the firm, unlined skin and clear, innocent eyes of youth anyhow? Nah. The crow's feet, worry lines, and cynical gaze of middle age were so much more appealing than the *tabula rasa* of twenty, I tried to convince myself. They hinted, after all, at lots seen and more done. Experience and all that. With a sigh I ran a comb through my hair, pleased that it was still auburn. Touching the swath of white hair over my left ear where a bullet had creased my scalp, I concluded that it gave me a raffish look. My eyes still had a steely greenish glint, my teeth were firm, white, and my own, and, no, I hadn't developed too many warts and wens. Not too bad, I decided. Fortysomething and holding. But holding what, my interior voice demanded. Holding up? Holding out? Holding on? And holding on for what?

I turned the hair blower up to HIGH and drowned out all such traitorous thoughts. Forty-something and holding. That was surely enough.

At precisely eight, showered, dressed, and more or less awake, I presented myself at my upstairs tenants' apartment. Wonderful smells of baking wafted out to meet me as Malcolm opened the door.

"Cinnamon buns?" I guessed hopefully.

"Righto," Malcolm replied. "And Oolong tea. Nice and strong."

"Er, great," I lied. I can't help it — I'm a coffee person. Tea in the morning just doesn't cut it. But Malcolm and his wife Yvonne *were* friends and they *had* asked me to breakfast. So I guessed I could suffer through a cup of tea for friendship's sake.

"So, how are things going at the shop?" I asked as I took a seat at the pine table in the kitchen eating alcove. The windows looked out on my tenants' dormant veggie garden and I noted with dismay that ominous piles of dark brown stuff were heaped here and there. No doubt some industrious tilling of the soil was about to take place. I made a mental note to go up-island the day the manure was delivered. Gardeners. They're so, well, *fanatical.* Making things grow approaches a religion with them. Sure, I like to thumb through seed catalogs as much as anyone, but I have no intention of actually digging in the dirt and *planting*. Think about it — once you've figured in the cost of shovels, rakes, hoes, trowels, fertilizer, stakes, ties, pest control, the gallons of water used, and your person-hours, you end up with the most expensive lettuce known to humankind. No, thanks. I'd rather just hustle on down to the corner market when I get a yen for salad. The local truck farmers do it far more cheaply. And worse than the cost is all that commitment — jeez, you might as well be married to your plot of dirt. If you're not watering, weeding or fretting, then you're seeking deliverance from some unimaginably repulsive and tenacious predator. Biology was never my favorite subject, so the less I know about the habits of the tomato hornworm or the grape leaf skeletonizer, the better. Still, pests do pose some interesting metaphysical questions. Why, for example, does the tomato hornworm ravage only tomatoes and not peppers? Very sporting of it. Is there a moral there for humankind? Fascinating.

"The shop? Oh, things are going great," Malcolm said, pushing a wing of blond hair out of his impossibly blue eyes. "I, er, that is, we, want to talk to you about something else."

"Well? Shoot."

"Um, well, you've been great to us — you loaned us the money to add the cafe to the shop, and you've never complained when our rent was late, but, well . . ." He trailed off and looked up at me, misery in his eyes.

"What is it, for God's sake?" I asked. "Is Yvonne ill?"

He shook his head.

"Are you?"

Another headshake.

"What, then?"

"I . . . Yvonne!" he called. "Will you come in here? I said I couldn't do this!"

I regarded him with amazement. What on earth was going on?

Behind me I heard Yvonne busy at the oven, and in a moment she came to join Malcolm, standing behind him and placing her hands on his shoulders. She bent down to kiss the top of his head and I remarked again how like brother and sister they looked — rosy-cheeked, blue-eyed, blonde, healthy. And right now, very worried.

"Caitlin, this is very embarrassing," she said. "After all your help, we feel, well, we're thinking of moving."

"What? Where?"

"Not far," she said. "Just out of town. We're thinking of buying a house. Well, a little farm, really. We could grow our own stuff for the cafe."

"Oh," I replied, feeling as though I'd just lost my best friends. Mal and Yvonne had lived upstairs for almost ten years. They were, well, family. But of course someday they'd want to move. Own something of their own. I resolved to put on a cheerful face. "Great. That's great. Where? Up-island?"

Looking relieved, Malcolm said, "No, up toward Sidney. Just off the Pat Bay Highway. A little ways north of Elk Lake." Leaping up, he said, "I'll get the cinnamon buns."

Yvonne took a seat at the table, tucked her hair behind her ears and looked up at me tentatively.

"We've loved living here," she said. "It's been very convenient. And you've been a great landlady. It's just that —"

"You want a place of your own," I provided.

"Yes."

"Buns are on the counter," Mal said. "I'm off to the cafe to get the soup ready." He came quickly to kiss me on the cheek. " 'Bye."

"We want to have a baby," Yvonne said after Mal had clattered down the stairs. She got up to put a plate of buns on the table. "We want to be living in our own home when we do."

"Oh," I said, biting into a cinnamon bun. Babies were not things I often thought about. "Sounds reasonable."

"We need to take some time away from the shop and the cafe," Yvonne said. "Hire a manager. Try to enjoy life. We're slaves to the place right now. If we do have a child, we have to arrange to have more free time."

"Good thinking," I told her. But already, I was selfishly worrying about my new tenants. God knows who I'd find. "Do you have a good realtor — someone who's helping you."

Yvonne nodded.

"Okay. Just be sensible. Don't pay too much."

She smiled. "We're just in the thinking stage. We won't do anything until we have all the facts."

"Good," I said, getting to my feet. "Listen, I have to go meet with a client. Thanks for the breakfast." I cleared the table, depositing plates and mugs in the sink, and took my jacket from the back of my chair. All this talk of babies and families and homes had depressed me. "Keep me posted, okay?"

"I will," she promised, disappointment in her eyes.

I closed the door softly, knowing I hadn't responded the way she'd wanted me to, and feeling irritated at her disappointment. Hey, give me a break!

On my way out of the McDonald's drive-through, large coffee in hand, I thought over what Yvonne had said about wanting a home and wanting to start a family. Well, why not? They were in their early thirties — still young enough. And a kid could do far worse than have them for parents. Still, the whole business depressed me and I felt small and mean about not feeling the joy Yvonne clearly intended I should. Shit. My problem was that I was too damned cat-like. I loathed change. I liked things to stay exactly the same in my life. Dammit. I downed the last of my coffee and tossed the empty cup over my shoulder into the back. The problem was, nothing ever stayed the same. Change, it seemed, was life's only constant.

I pulled into Laura's and Liz's driveway in James Bay at exactly five minutes to nine. A green truck was parked in front of what had to be the world's smallest, whitest bungalow. The truck was loaded with well-used but fastidiously maintained gardening equipment — a mower, edgers, shovels, rakes, and clippers, and a garbage pail and a few bags of redwood bark. The whole works was contained in a kind of metal cage built on the back of the pickup. Walking behind it, I noted that the license plate read 4 U I MOW. I smiled. I guessed that when Liz wasn't worried to death about Laura she had quite a sense of humor.

Liz met me at the front door, brown envelope in hand. "She left a list for you," she informed me. "And photos and stuff. It's all in here."

"Left it?" I began to do a slow burn.

"Yeah. She figured she'd feel better if she went in to work today. Besides, she has a class at the detention facility later this afternoon and I guess those guys really get bent out of shape if she misses."

Bent out of shape? Laura didn't know the meaning of the phrase. When I got finished with her she'd resemble a pretzel. "Why do I get the impression your other half isn't exactly being cooperative? The two of you say you want my help, but it seems that the help has to be on Laura's terms. There's a teeny power struggle going on here, *n'est ce pas?*"

Liz said nothing, her face sullen.

"Oh, c'mon Liz, help me out a little, will you? Is she like this about everything, or is it just me?"

"No," Liz said, "it's not just you."

"Well, that's good to know."

"I'd ask you in," Liz said, "but I have lawns waiting. The pictures are just inside. On the coffee table. I'll get them."

The screen door snapped shut after her. I leaned on the porch rail, watching a robin hop across the lawn, cocking its head every now and then, listening for worms. In a moment, Liz returned, a fat brown envelope in her hands. I took it from her.

"Give me directions to the place where Laura works."

"It's just off Lochside, opposite the park. The next driveway after the private boys' academy. Willows Art Magnet School. You're not going to, well . . ." She looked at me, distress in her eyes.

"What? Rant and rave? No, I'm not going to rant and rave. I just need to talk to her." *But I may wring her neck,* I added silently as I hurried down the steps to my car.

A trio of boys about fifteen with floppy hair and baggy clothes sat on a bench just beyond the parking lot of Willows Art Magnet School, giggling over a magazine. To my dismay, I realized that the school was nothing more than a collection of portables, none bearing signs. I could wander around here all day and still not find what I wanted. Shit. I was in no mood for wandering.

"Excuse me," I said to the guffawing trio. "Where's the administration office?"

One of the boys, a blond, looked up momentarily, then resumed his perusal of the magazine. The other two ignored me completely.

"Great ass," a still-childish tenor voice said. "Fabulous tits, too."

That did it. I ripped the magazine out of their grasp, rolled it into a tube and whacked the vocal junior lecher across the ears with it. He fell off the bench into a rhododendron bush where he gazed up at me in open-mouthed amazement.

"Hey!" he said, his manly dignity affronted. "That's my property!"

"No kidding? I bet it's required reading, too."

His friends snickered nervously. I silenced them with a glare.

"Let's do this again," I said. "I'll say it real slow because what with you guys being gifted arts students and all, you're probably not too left-brained. Where's the administration office?"

Lecher, on his butt in the rhodie bush, briefly contemplated a smart-ass reply, thought better of it, and tossed his head sullenly. "The first building on the left," he managed.

"Good," I told him. "Real good. Now get your asses back to class."

They shuffled to their feet, Lecher muttering under his breath.

"Now!" I roared.

To my surprise, they went. Gee whiz, Caitlin old girl, I congratulated myself, you haven't lost your touch, have you? You can still frighten fifteen-year-olds, just like you did when you were a teacher. And probably old folks and infirm dogs, too, I thought. Yup, you're a real terror. Well, let's see how well you do with Laura. Heck, if all else fails, you can beat her about the head and shoulders with the boys' magazine. I unrolled it, noted to my disgust that it was an old issue of *Hustler,* and heaved it at the nearest garbage can. Wiping my hands on my jeans, I strode off in the direction of the administration office.

* * * * *

"Not here? What do you mean she's not here?" I asked the fiftyish, frizzy-haired clerk in the admin office. "Is she out doing an errand or out on a field trip or out contemplating her navel by the seashore? What exactly does 'not here' mean?" I was tired of ambiguous answers and fresh out of patience. Why the hell can't people say what they mean? God, we do enough talking these days, but half of it is meaningless. Maybe more.

The clerk raised her eyebrows. "Well now, I don't know if I can give you that information," she said archly, prepared to engage in the Bureaucratic Obstructionist Two-Step with me.

"It's either me or the police, Tootsie Pop," I told her, tossing my card on the counter. "I'm working for Ms. Neal. I expected to find her here. I have reason to believe she may be in danger. If you know where she is, you tell me now, or I call the cops."

"Oh? Danger, you say?" I noted that instead of concern, an avid curiosity filled her eyes. She all but licked her chops. "Well, Laura *did* phone about seven this morning to say that she wouldn't be in today."

The bottom fell out of my stomach. Jesus Christ. What was going on here? "Do you have a pay phone?"

"In the hall." She gestured. "But you can use mine if you like." Her eyes positively sparkled.

Oh, sure. "The hall will be fine," I told her.

I hadn't wanted to do things this way, but events were forcing my hand. I hurried to my car, retrieved the one flimsy sheet of yellow lined paper that reposed in the brown envelope Liz had pressed on me, added it to the list Laura had made last night, and hurried back into the admin building. In the hall I dug in my pocket for some change and dialed the number for Theo's apartment. The phone rang seven times and I seethed through every ring. Of course he won't be there, idiot, I told myself. He's probably moved long ago. Flown the coop. To my surprise, the phone was answered on the eighth ring.

"Mmmmp?" a sleepy voice grunted.

I was so taken aback, I just asked, "Is Theo Blalock there?"

"Nah." Big yawn. "Zatwork."

Jesus, talk about luck. I ran my finger down the list until I came to Theo's last known place of employment. "Um, at the cannery?"

"Mmmhmmm."

"Thanks."

I hung up and sprinted for the parking lot.

This was too easy, I thought as I drove over the bridge to Esquimalt and the Pan Pacific Cannery. Way too easy. What in hell was I paying the Ferret an exorbitant hourly rate for if Theo was, well, just hanging around. Why, Laura had . . . I tapped my fingers on the wheel. Yes, indeedy, Laura had led me to believe that she had no idea where her ex was. And presto, I found him just like that? As those two idiot countrymen of mine are so fond of saying on TV: "Not!" Hmmm.

As I crested the hill and sped down the other side to the ocean, the presence of cannery hit me like a slap in the face with a cold cod. In a word, it stank. No wonder it was stuck out of town on a promontory where the ocean breezes could blow the odor of fish guts away. Far away. Whew! I bet real estate prices downwind from this baby were very reasonable indeed.

I wheeled into the parking lot, found a place for my MG, and hurried to the building marked OFFICE. Once inside, I fished in my wallet for one of my phoney business cards — this time the one that identified me as C.R. Reece, Island Insurance Investigations. Very respectable.

Approaching the front counter, I caught the eye of a pretty young redhead in a too-tight pink sweater and black pants.

"Theo Blalock," I said with my widest smile. "Is he at work today?" I gave Pink Sweater my card.

"Um, well, I'd have to check," she said uncertainly.

"Would you do that? Theo's going to be one mighty happy guy," I told her confidentially, lowering my voice.

"Oh yeah?"

"Uh huh. That accident he was involved in? Well, it was definitely the other guy's fault. Theo's going to collect a ton of money."

"Oh yeah?" she repeated, vacant blue eyes open wide. I groaned. Oh goody. A zoid.

"So will you check?" I urged her.

"Check?"

I prayed for forbearance. "On whether Theo's at work today? I want to be able to tell him the good news."

"Oh. Yeah. I can do that." She turned to riffle through a display of time cards. "Oops. Like, he was here, for about an hour this morning. But he clocked out just after eight."

Dammit. "Oh well," I said, trying to sound nonchalant. "I guess he got sick or something."

"It better not be 'or something,' " Pink Sweater said. "The boss'll fire his ass if he takes any more time off over that old lady of his."

"Oh?" I tried not to show how interested I was.

"Yeah." She frowned. "That broad is, like, a mental case or something."

"His old lady — that would be Laura, right?" I held my breath.

"Yeah, Laura. Skinny, washed-out-looking blonde," she said, fluffing her own blazing curls. "She's like, crazy about him, I guess. Or maybe she's just plain crazy. Anyhow, she won't leave him alone."

"Oh?" I said, feigning ignorance.

"Well, they're separated, y'know," Pink Sweater said. "Hey, I hope that means she won't get her hands on any of that money you were talking about. Anyhow, that woman's a big pain in the rear end."

"Oh yeah?" Jeez. I was starting to sound like Pink Sweater.

"Yeah. Lately, she's been phoning about once a week. She's even come down here twice."

"Oh yeah?"

She nodded. "Yeah. They'd go out in the parking lot and yell at each other."

"Hmmm. I wonder what about."

She winked. "Another guy."

My mouth about fell open. "Another . . . guy?"

"Sure. I guess Theo caught her with some guy and booted her out." She shrugged. "Now she wants to come back and Theo's saying 'No way, Jose.' " She giggled gleefully.

"Oh, so you heard them talking about this?"

"Well, not exactly. Theo told me." She smirked. Oh sure, I thought. That sounded like just the kind of fairy tale a red-blooded he-man would invent to hide the fact that his wife preferred another woman to him. After all, a guy has to be able to tell his co-workers something. But what were they yelling at each other about, I wondered.

"Deena!" a furious voice yelled from an office down the hall.

"Gotta go," she said cheerfully. "Want me to tell Theo you called?"

"Nah, I'll catch him at home," I told her. "Thanks anyhow."

"No problem."

I walked back to my car in a fog of confusion. What the hell was going on here? I wasn't sure, but I was beginning to get the feeling that someone was playing me for a sucker. I couldn't for the life of me fathom how, or why, but if it proved to be true, I was going to do a little yelling of my own. Well, things would come clear soon enough. In the meantime, just in case I was wrong about this sucker business, I thought I'd better learn all I could about Theo Blalock.

Intent on clearing the stink of fish guts from my nose, I rolled the windows down and reveled in the cold clean Pacific air. Fish. Yechh. Maybe I'd become a vegetarian after all.

I stopped for gas just outside town and made a quick call to my friend Sandy, a.k.a. Detective

Sergeant Gary Alexander of the Oak Bay Police Department. I had a few things I wanted to run by him.

"Alexander," he rumbled.

"Hey, Sandy, how about lunch?"

"Caitlin!" he exclaimed in delight. "Lunch, aye, I can manage lunch. Are you buying?"

"Not on your life. You eat enough for a whole hurling team. No, we'll go Dutch."

"Och, how you do malign me. All right, then. How about twelve fifteen at The Pub in the Oak Bay Beach Hotel."

"You're on. And just so you're warned, I want to pick your brain."

"About?"

"A guy named Theo Blalock. Ring any bells?"

"Hmmm. No. But I'll run his name through our wee electronic beastie downstairs and see what we've got."

That was just what I'd hoped he'd do. "Great. See you at lunch."

The Oak Bay Beach Hotel is a huge black and white Tudor edifice clinging to an intimate, rocky crescent beach. It's old-fashioned and homey inside and usually I find it soothing. Today, however, it just seemed gloomy. Probably a function of my mood. I had fallen into a funk during my drive back into town from the fish cannery and now felt depressed and morose. Still, the views out to sea were terrific, I admitted, as I took a window table in The Pub. From where I sat, I could look out to sea and drown my sorrows while watching the sun trying its very best to make the billows smooth and bright, as Lewis Carroll said. I had hardly started on the sorrow-drowning when Sandy found me.

"Guinness," he told the waitress who showed him to my table.

"Oh God, Alexander, how can you drink that stuff?"

"Ha! It's far better for you than that mare's urine you're drinking," he said, indicating my glass of straw-colored draft beer.

"You could well be right," I said, downing my Labatt's. "I'm really not much of a beer drinker. It just seems like the thing to do in here."

"Hmmf," he said, lowering his considerable bulk into the chair opposite mine.

"You're looking good," I told him. And he was. Although he's over six feet and probably weighs close to 250 pounds, he carries it well. An enthusiastic rugby player, he'd knocked heads with other amateurs in a weekend league for as long as I can remember.

"Kind of you to say so," he said, smoothing his moustache and adjusting the lapels of his tweed sports jacket a little self-consciously. He looked up at me from under bushy, sand-colored eyebrows. "You're looking, well, comfortable."

I laughed out loud. "Comfortable? Yes, I suppose I am." I remembered my days at the Crown Prosecutor's office when I dressed in obligatory wool suits, pearls, and imported leather shoes. God, how I'd hated all that. Nowadays I wore jeans, turtlenecks, my dad's well-worn bomber jacket, and running shoes. And loved it. For really special occasions, I had a Fair Isle vest, a Harris Tweed blazer, a pair of camel wool pants, and some loafers. But that outfit was comfortable, too. I just wasn't into suffering anymore.

We ordered lunch — a beef and kidney pie for Sandy and fish and chips for me — and while we waited, I filled him in on what I needed.

"Well, your Theo Blalock hasn't exactly been a good boy," he said, reaching into an inner pocket of his blazer and drawing out a computer printout, "but he isn't Al Capone, either. Here's his sheet."

I read it over quickly. The usual parking tickets and speeding tickets. A couple of arrests for bar fights. More interesting, two complaints filed against him by his wife, Laura. But neither of these had ever come to trial.

"What gives?" I asked Sandy. "Is this what I think it is — the old He Beats Me Therefore He Loves Me thing?"

He dabbed his moustache delicately with a paper napkin. "Could be."

I scanned Theo's sheet again. "He does seem to enjoy using his fists."

"I asked around," Sandy said. "Blalock is a type. A scrapper. He's a wee fellow — about your size. Wiry, too. Seems to think he has something to prove. Ruth Edgall, one of our constables, has answered more than one call to the Queen's Arms to break up fights in which Mr. Blalock was involved. She had to wrestle him to the floor one time to cuff him. He's never forgiven her for that. Ruth could probably tell you a lot about him. And about the wife, too." He cleared his throat meaningfully.

"I know what you're thinking, Alexander," I told

him. "I'm kinda thinking the same thing myself — that this present nonsense with the photos is just another scene in the Theo and Laura Follies. I'd like to think that the two of them are just playing domestic games. But somehow . . ." I trailed off and looked out at the slate blue water. A few brave sailboats were scudding before the wind, white wings spread against a dove gray sky. "This seems too elaborate. Too . . . indirect for someone who solves his problems by using his fists. Besides, Laura says Theo's not involved."

"Hmmmf," Sandy said, eloquently expressing his opinion on that subject.

"Yeah, maybe," I agreed. "But look — she's filed complaints on him before. She's acknowledged that he's been abusive. Why would she maintain he wasn't sending the photos if she knew darned well he was? For that matter, why hire me to find out who's doing it if she knows it's Theo?"

"Well," Sandy rumbled, "whether he's doing this or not, according to Ruth Edgall, he's a nasty little fellow."

I sighed. Why is it that these bastards hold such a fascination for some women?

Sandy swallowed the rest of his Guinness and stroked his moustache thoughtfully. "You know, about this photo thing, I've had a thought. I know a woman . . ." He paused. "Metro Vancouver's used her in the past, and so has the R.C.M.P. She's been immensely useful and right on the money."

"Useful for what?"

"She's a psychological profiler. Has a couple of degrees — criminology, psychology — worked for a while at Quantico with the FBI. She's written at least one book. Teaches this stuff, too. So she's very well qualified. Anyhow, when she was working with Metro Van, oh, seven or eight years ago I think it was, I had occasion to meet her. And I think I recall . . ." He frowned, massaging his brow as if to force information out. "A case that involved photos." Finally he shook his head. "If you like, I could ask her to talk to you."

"You mean, someone, what, seven or eight years ago, was doing what Theo's doing to Laura. Scaring women by sending photo collages?"

"Something of the sort."

I sat back, mystified. Seven or eight years ago Theo Blalock had been in high school. Still . . . "Sure, I'd like to talk to her if she has the time."

He drummed his fingers on the tabletop. "She's . . . a difficult person. I can't guarantee she'll see you. But I suppose I could give her a call."

Sandy was gone for about three minutes — hardly enough time for me to give this any coherent thought. When he returned, his face bore an odd, sad smile. "She said yes," he informed me, signaling the waitress. "Dessert?" he asked. "The trifle is exceptionally good here."

Trifle? I groaned. I'd have to swim an extra fifty laps to work off dessert. "Let me have a few bites of yours." I told the waitress, "I'll have coffee, though."

"What's up?" I asked him when the waitress had gone to fetch our orders.

"Hmmm?" he replied innocently.

"Come off it, Alexander, we know each other too well for this. What's up?"

He sighed. "I'd best be honest with you. Eliane St. Cyr — the woman I'm sending you to see — hasn't been actively working for quite a few years. She won't go out in the field anymore — says she prefers to write and teach."

"So?"

"So she's hiding," he said quietly. "I tell her that every time I talk to her, which is about once a year for five minutes."

"Hiding from what?"

"Ah, now that's the question, isn't it?"

I raised an eyebrow. Sandy and this Eliane woman? A couple? Ye gods — I would have been willing to bet that here was one man who'd never been unfaithful to his wife. Still, anything was possible.

"You can stifle that thought," he told me, reading my mind.

I actually blushed. "Sorry. So what's the big deal? Can't she retire if she wants?"

He peered at me from the thicket of his eyebrows. "Caitlin, the woman isn't fifty. That's a little young for retirement."

"Hmmm. Well, I'm sure she has her reasons." Then comprehension dawned. "Why, Sergeant Alexander, are you asking me to be a spy? An informant? I'm surprised at you."

He sighed. "Aye, maybe I am. She's so . . . evasive." He looked at me fiercely, blue eyes ablaze. "We need her, Caitlin. Us, the thin blue line, we need this woman. Her insights were nothing short of uncanny." He sighed again. "And a lot of us supported her theory. It was an interesting one —

that we could derail a lot of potential serial killers and mass murderers by looking at the psych profiles and arrest records of youthful offenders. If it could work, it would certainly save everyone a lot of grief."

"Interesting idea," I admitted. "But how would it work? What would we do — lock the monsters up while they're still juvies? Get their heads shrunk? Try to make them see the error of their ways." I snorted. "That's been tried. There are cartloads of books written on identification of delinquent behavior and its possible treatment. And none of it works worth a rat's ass."

He shook his head. "I agree. Of course all that claptrap doesn't work. But Eliane wasn't interested in rehabilitation of juvenile offenders. Just their identification." He toyed with his teaspoon. "I'd certainly appreciate knowing who we ought to keep closer tabs on. A system like hers could help us a lot." He smiled at a private memory.

I thought about this for a moment. Hell, it could work. "A police department might well want to know who its potential big-time offenders were likely to be."

He nodded. "She did interviews, developed a good theoretical model. In practical terms, though, I don't know if she ever cracked the nut of how to access juvenile records. They're sealed."

"Probably not. You know how touchy the courts are about that. Of course she could get the information she wanted from different sources."

He raised his eyebrows.

"You know, court-appointed psychologists, sociologists, physicians, school officials, church pastors, teachers — heck, I can think of a dozen different ways to do it besides butting heads with the juvie court folks." I thought about Francis the Ferret. "And then there's always the wonderful world of electronic snooping."

"Ah, but then it wouldn't be official, would it?" he asked rhetorically.

"I see," I said at length. "She went as far as she could in developing this system but it, what, failed, because there was no way it could bear the system's papal seal? Give me a break!"

He shrugged.

"Hey, there's something wrong here. If her system can identify potential adult criminals — the rapists, the arsonists, the child molesters, the serial murderers — it seems to me that there ought to be some way it could be made official."

"Seems logical," he said, fiddling with the teaspoon again.

I sat back and looked at him. There was something going on, something swimming just beneath the surface of our conversation that worried me. "So what happened to her, to Eliane?" I asked.

"Several years ago, when she was working with Metro Van, she traded them her expertise in catching the Zoo Murderer for access to their computer files on youthful offenders."

"You worked on the Zoo Murders? I never knew that."

He grimaced. "Aye. It was just before I applied for a transfer to Oak Bay."

A transfer? I sensed there was a volume, if not a trilogy, waiting to be written here but decided to sidestep the subject for the time being. "So, what happened? Did she get what she wanted — the data?"

"Yes. I know she did because she told me. She was excited. She started to work with files, conducted interviews with the young scum — in prison and out — and then, all of a sudden, she just quit. The Zoo Murderer had been caught by then and she just packed up and went to Switzerland, of all places."

Without saying goodbye to you, Alexander, I bet. "Well, obviously something happened," I concluded.

"I thought so, too," he said quietly. "But she says no, every time I ask. Claims that she just wants to —"

"Write and teach. Right."

We sat in silence for a few moments.

"I'll go see her," I told him after a bit. "And if the occasion arises for me to ask about the work she left, I'll do it."

"Thank you," he said, unable to meet my eyes. Jesus, I thought, he can deny it all he wants, but he's got it bad for this broad.

The trifle arrived at precisely that moment.

"Oh my God," I groaned, making a fuss to lighten the mood. "I'll have to buy a whole new wardrobe after this."

"Ha! As if you'll get more than the few bites you asked for!"

We laughed and dug into the dessert, but underneath our gaiety, something was different. I felt that something between us had changed shape, that our relationship had been altered in some subtle, yet fundamental way, and realizing this made me sadder than I would have thought possible. God, here was another change. I realized with a jolt that Sandy was one of the few people in my life I had felt I could absolutely count on, one of my inner circle of friends and sustainers. Now he, too, had restructured the terms of our relationship. Dammit, was nothing immutable?

Chapter 6

As I negotiated the coast highway on my way to Eliane St. Cyr's, I found myself feeling more than a bit testy. Perhaps it was the buildup Sandy had given her or perhaps it was the fact that I had been granted a couple hours of her time only as a favor to him. I loathe being a supplicant. Caitlin Reece, mendicant. I snorted. When I worked for the CP I always dealt from a position of power — I had information to trade, favors to bestow, deals to make. In private work, though, things were different. Over the past few years, I'd done enough equivocating, dissembling, and downright lying to last me a lifetime. Not to mention breaking half a dozen laws. Acting outside the law doesn't thrill me, but sometimes it's necessary. Knowledge, which is, after all, the key to power, is an elusive commodity. At the CP's office I was cloaked in the authority of The Law. I could require that people talk to me. Now, I go naked in the world with only my wits, imagination, and determination to serve me. No one is required to tell me anything, so I have to figure out how best to extract the facts I need. Some people require persuasion, some a sympathetic ear, some a bit of forceful insistence. The trick is discovering which technique will work.

What about Eliane? I wondered. She might well be the greatest living expert on psychological profiling of criminals, but could she really tell me anything in the hour I'd been granted with her? And I had to admit that, dammit, I was nervous. I was about to meet an Important Person and I was dressed in my jeans and Reeboks. Ah well, I'd have to let my wit and charm make the impression, not my Levi's and sneakers.

I cruised into Sidney at quarter to three, and found Oceanside Drive without any problem. Set well back from the street, big, rambling one-story houses sat on half-acre lots crowded with evergreens and rhododendrons. Every lawn looked scrupulously well-manicured. I guessed that these homes had been built in the fifties or early sixties — the houses themselves were nothing special but the land they sat on must now be worth a fortune. Behind the houses, backyards sloped sharply to the sea and I bet each one had a fabulous view of the channel.

Eleven forty sat at the end of a cul-de-sac, and I drove by it twice before I realized that it wasn't a small hotel or a large B & B but was, indeed, the house I sought. It was a pretty remarkable edifice — two stories of stone and redwood set on at least three lots, with a detached garage as big as my house and a carriage house nestled in back amid a mini-forest of madrones. Impressive was an understatement. The criminal-profiling business must be more lucrative than I'd thought.

I wheeled my ancient MG slowly into the driveway, parked, and ascended the stone steps to the massive double front door. Solid oak, I thought, as I traced the raised door panels with one finger. I raised the knocker and let it fall. Then I waited. The cold spring air was full of the scent of earth, cedar, and the sea, and I tried to rustle up a little enthusiasm. No dice. After a few moments, a sturdy gray-haired woman in a black dress cracked the door.

"Eliane St. Cyr?"

She looked me up and down appraisingly, then shook her head. No smile. "*Non, mademoiselle.* I'm Agathe, Dr. St. Cyr's housekeeper. You are . . . ?"

I sighed. How many people was the good doctor expecting today, anyhow? "Reece. Caitlin Reece."

"Ah. The investigator," Agathe said, making it sound, well, sordid. "Come in. She's in the sitting room at the back of the house. I'm just about to serve tea. We waited for you," she added, a note of reproach in her voice.

"Thanks," I said coolly.

I followed Agathe's ample form down a wide

flagstone corridor that smelled of furniture polish, past half a dozen closed doors, until we reached the back of the house. She motioned for me to precede her and as I entered the room, I gasped. It wasn't a sitting room, it was a mini-library. A high ceiling accommodated twelve- or fourteen-foot-high bookcases which were absolutely packed with books, periodicals, and bulging file folders. On the stone floor was a huge Oriental carpet in an intricate weave of crimson, cobalt, black and white. Two cobalt tweed sofas flanked the fireplace, a coffee table that I guessed was ebony between them. At one end of the sofa, her back to the window, sat a woman, and it took me a moment to tear my greedy eyes from the room to her. How could I have not noticed her immediately? She seemed tall, probably taller than I, thin and angular, with sleek dark hair drawn severely back from her face and tied in a knot at the nape of her neck. She was elegantly dressed in what looked like a white silk shirt with a cashmere turtleneck underneath it and black wool pants. Her face was a pale oval in the gloom but I got an impression of straight black eyebrows, a small straight nose and dark, dark eyes. The face of an aristocrat.

At the moment, however, she was evidently in another world — the world of music. Rich, slightly disharmonic sounds filled the room and it took me a moment to realize what was playing — the last part of "The House on Hen's Legs" from Mussorgsky's *Pictures at an Exhibition,* the powerful sequence that concludes the frantic flight from Baba Yaga, the evil witch. Atop all that orchestral complexity, the composer had overlaid the theme of the next piece, "The Great Gate at Kiev." I love this piece of music, probably because I first heard it as a very young teenager, hungry for voices that spoke to my soul, voices more eloquent than those I heard daily on the local rock or country and western radio stations. It was my freshman year of high school and someone had decided that music appreciation would be a good idea. I don't know how much the other kids got out of the class — taught by a painfully earnest young blonde woman named, appropriately, Miss Carol — but "The Great Gate at Kiev," Pachelbel's "Canon and Fugue," Ravel's "Bolero," Purcell's "Dido and Aeneas" all spoke to me in a way that nothing else ever had. And so I stood rooted to the spot as the sheer power of this piece reached out and took me once again by the throat. For a moment the room, the woman I had come to see, everything, dropped away as the music riveted me, peeling my senses so that I stood defenseless, waiting for what I knew would follow. Hearing this piece of music after a long time away from it seems to me like making love after a long period of celibacy — the power always amazes. *What an odd coincidence that this stranger should share my taste in music,* I thought with my last shred of rationality, just before my soul was wrenched out of my body and tossed like a winged thing into the maelstrom of the music. I knew that, heedless of what my hostess might think, I had to just close my eyes and *feel.* The piece lasted an eternity, it lasted an instant, but suddenly it was over and there was only the static hiss of tape. The woman on the couch raised what I guessed to be a remote control, clicked it, and then that sound, too, died.

In the silence, I cleared my throat, hoping I would be able to speak.

"Someone I know said that sex is humans' closest approximation to ecstasy," the woman said. "I disagree. I think it's music. What do you think?"

"Me?" I managed to say after I'd recovered from my surprise. "I agree with you. I think music is the closest we'll come to ecstasy."

She smiled and held out a hand. "I think so, too. Miss Reece? I'm Eliane St. Cyr." To my surprise, she didn't rise or walk toward me. *What gives,* I wondered, feeling as though I must have missed a cue.

"Please, Caitlin will do," I said, walking around the end of the sofa toward her, trying to place her accent. I stopped and held out my hand to her, expecting her to take mine, to rise and meet me halfway, but she sat immobile, her hand still outstretched, the same smile on her lips, her eyes focused . . . on nothing. *God, she's blind,* I realized suddenly, feeling like a fool. I walked to her, put my hand in hers and she closed both her hands over mine, pressing it warmly.

"There," she said. "You have good hands. Strong."

I mumbled something and she laughed.

"Here, sit where you can see the ocean." She gestured to the sofa across from her. "I will stay here in my favorite spot while we talk."

"Um," I cleared my throat, "thank you for seeing me. I understand you're very busy and I appreciate it." But busy with exactly what, I wondered. Sandy had said she was consulting on a case for another agency but I wondered how. I mean, police work is nothing if it isn't reading.

"When Sandy called, I gave Romany the afternoon off. Romany's my assistant," she explained. "Since my . . . accident, she's been my eyes."

"Oh," I said, wondering if I was supposed to inquire or ignore. "What happened?" I asked, deciding on the former.

"What happened? A jest of God. Optic nerve damage," she told me evasively. "My vision's been deteriorating for about eight years." She shrugged one elegant shoulder. "I can see shapes, blurs, distinguish light from dark. But soon, I fear, I will be able to see nothing at all."

"Isn't there any treatment available?" I asked, horrified.

"Oh, there's something radical being pioneered in Switzerland, but nothing here on this continent."

"Tea," Agathe announced from the doorway. She placed the tray down in the center of the table and with another appraising glance at me, left us alone again. I was surprised when Eliane leaned forward, her hands searching the tray, lightly locating its contents. Then, to my greater surprise, she lifted the teapot and poured two cups of tea. "Help yourself to cream or sugar," she said. "I hope you like this. It's Jubilee Blend. Perfect for a gloomy afternoon, don't you think? And do have one of Agathe's shortbreads. They're marvelous."

I nibbled, admiring the fine clean lines of the china cups and the fine clean lines of Eliane's profile. With the afternoon light behind her, her face was shadowed, mysterious. How did she work without her sight, I wondered. What did the indispensable Romany do for her? She put her teacup down on the table, sat back, and smoothed her glossy hair with one pale hand. Then she turned to face me, stretching one arm along the back of the sofa, fingers caressing the nubbly material. The movement drew her shirt tight against her breasts and I had a moment's moral dilemma: to ogle or not to ogle. Certainly Eliane wouldn't know. I sighed. I just couldn't do it. I'd feel too much like a voyeur. Instead, I turned my admiration to the library.

"What are you thinking about?" she asked after a moment.

"How . . . beautiful everything is," I said honestly. "This room . . . the furnishings . . . the view." *And you,* I added silently. *And you.*

"Oh, thank you," she said, seemingly taken aback. "Well, let's begin, shall we? Sandy explained the salient aspects of the case to me on the phone. His memory serves him correctly. The affair I was involved with several years ago bears enough similarities to your case that I asked Sandy to send you to me. It's possible that your burglar and my offender could be the same man."

I tried not to get excited. "Your guy did what — sent photos to women?"

"Yes. Collages of their own photos. Photos he'd taken from their houses."

Bingo. It was Theo Blalock — it had to be! "Why'd he send the photos?" I asked, excited. "What did he want?"

"We never discovered that," she said. "Martin was

jailed for assault — a separate charge — before he'd ever made any demands of his victims. Or gone any further."

"Wait — Martin?"

"Yes, Martin Fell. My burglar."

My heart sank. "My guy's name is Theo Blalock."

She waved her hand. "A minor inconsistency. Names are easily changed."

"Mmmm. Maybe. But what did you mean, 'gone any further'?"

"What did Sandy tell you about me?" she asked, dodging the question.

I shrugged. "Not much. Only that you were a criminologist with an interest in juvenile offenders."

"That's basically correct," she said. "I began my career studying abnormal psychology, but realized soon enough that I was going down the wrong path. You see, I've always had an interest — a curiosity, if you will — in the dark side of human nature. About what makes men monsters. Because you know, there are monsters." She turned her dark eyes on me and I swallowed convulsively. "That's really why you're here, isn't it? That's why Sandy sent you to me. You think — no, you *feel* — that you have a monster on your hands."

I tried to speak but my mouth was suddenly too dry to answer. Monsters. I sat rooted to the spot, dumb, as a starburst exploded in my brain illuminating a room I had kept dark most of my life. The room in which I kept my own monster memorabilia — Marc Bergeron's delighted answer to my query about why he did the things he did: "Because I can." Baxter Buchanan's giddy glee as he was about to pull the trigger and send me to oblivion. The hot rage that had looked out of Kirk Ratliffe's eyes from the time he was a teenager. Monsters. And, in another flash of insight, I realized that hidden in my brain's secret room was my own private monster — someone from my past, someone who waited for me in the cellar, in the dark at the foot of the stairs. Someone whose name I almost knew . . . someone whose face I could almost see —

"Do you?" Eliane asked, interrupting my epiphany. I blinked, trying to return to this room and this woman, to the present, to sanity, to safety.

"Do I what?" I asked, my voice husky with emotion.

"Have a monster on your hands?"

"I . . . I . . . didn't think so," I croaked, then cleared my throat and carried on. "I was hoping that this might be nothing more serious than a case of a husband who can't let his woman go. Not that that's not serious," I amended. "But a monster?" I felt the hair lift on the back of my neck. Not another one, I prayed. Not yet. I'm not ready.

"The study of these men, of these monsters, is a hard thing," she said. "In classes I've taught, big tough cops have broken down and wept. After we review cases, many of them are unable to sleep at night. Your voice tells me of your distress. Please don't be ashamed. Distress affirms your humanity. This is what makes us different from the monsters."

"Yes, well," I muttered. But I was embarrassed all the same. Ashamed. Hadn't I seen enough horrors in the Crown Prosecutor's office to make me pretty thick-skinned? Dammit, I had. So what was wrong with me, going into a fugue like that? I was acting like a civilian, like someone's maiden aunt, for God's sake.

"Tell me about your case," she invited.

"Well, at this point, I haven't much to tell," I said, and in a few moments, outlined the facts as I knew them. "I can't find the husband," I said in frustration, "the ex-wife is deliberately avoiding me, and the lover is foaming at the mouth she's so upset about all this."

"Mmmm. You've considered extortion?"

"Yeah." I remembered with a start that it was in fact Laura who had articulated the idea. Strange.

"Does either of the women have any money?"

"Liz does."

She was silent for a moment. "Yes, extortion is a logical assumption. That is, if the burglar wants anything that can be logically understood."

"Right. And so far he hasn't asked for anything. He just sends the photos." Eliane said nothing, so I continued. "Then there's Liz's theory that it's Theo trying to frighten Laura back to him."

"It's certainly a possibility," she said. "It seems rather . . . convoluted for a scare tactic, though."

"Yeah, it does."

"So that leaves you where?"

I sighed. "Who knows? It's a little too soon to tell."

"There is another explanation," she offered. "The reason why Sandy sent you to me."

My stomach clenched. "This monster thing?"

"Yes." She was silent for a moment. "Shall we speculate about monsters, Miss Reece?"

"Caitlin," I said automatically. "Miss Reece makes me feel like I'm still teaching freshman English."

"Caitlin, then. Well?"

I really wanted to say, *No, the last thing in the world I want to talk about is monsters. Please, no, I have done battle with monsters and been defeated. Monsters have hurt me grievously, monsters have almost killed me.* But something held me tongue-tied. Why couldn't I just say no? What prevented me from declining this look into the pit? To my dismay, I found myself casually agreeing. "Okay. Let's speculate."

"The burglary in which the photo album was taken — was anything else stolen?"

"I haven't gotten around to asking," I said.

"When you do, inquire whether items such as underwear were taken."

"Underwear?"

"This sounds like a fetish burglary. Photos are very intimate things. So are letters and trophies. Items of clothing such as underwear fall into this category too. Also perfume and cosmetics. What I would look for if I were you is whether several personal items were stolen."

Oh brother, I thought.

"If this is a fetish burglary, it's most likely the first stage in what's going to be a sex crime."

"What? A sex crime? How can you possibly know?"

She smiled bitterly. "There are few things in this world that I know for certain, but this is one of them. I know. This is what I spent almost twenty years of my life developing — the identification of behaviors that predict these horrible crimes. Particularly the serial crimes."

"Behaviors?"

She exhaled heavily. "These men — and they are mostly always men — don't just wake up one morning and commit mayhem. Oh no. Each one leaves signs, tracks, if you will, a trail, that winds through his family, his peers, his church, his school experiences, his visits to doctors and psychologists, his early brushes with the law. If you know what to look for — and I do — these signs fairly shout at you. They're crimson threads running through gray lives."

"And fetish burglaries are one of these threads?"

"Definitely. You see, if the theft was an act of fetishism, then no, it wasn't 'just a burglary.' Why not? Because the perpetrator stole items which are necessary to the creation of a fantasy — a fantasy to which only he knows the script."

She didn't need any prompting to continue.

"This is a fantasy which he has been creating in his mind for years. Since childhood, most likely," she said. "And it's typical of these kinds of offenders that the older they get, the greater is their need to live out their fantasy."

"How do you mean?"

She smiled, a rueful, sad smile. "By forcing a woman, usually someone they know, to participate in the fantasy with them. You see, they've been obsessively imagining all the details of the fantasy for years, building it the way a novelist will build a story, adding on chapters, if you will, except for one essential thing. The ending."

"The ending? You mean they don't know it?"

"I really don't think they do," Eliane said. "For

years they've been playing and replaying a ritualized inner script — one which they've very carefully developed. But no, they really don't know its ending."

"What kind of script?"

"Okay. Here's an example. John Cheney was a postal worker — a letter carrier. Mousy young man. Quiet. No friends. Lived with his mother. One day he forced his way into the home of a young woman on his route and murdered her. Her body was found laid out on her bed, hands clasped over her breasts, makeup freshly applied, clothes folded neatly on a nearby chair. She had been strangled. But before death she had been bitten quite severely on her breasts." She shifted slightly, as though the story made her uncomfortable. "All these acts were very meaningful parts of his fantasy. With these kinds of killers they always are." She cleared her throat. "Cheney did this several more times before we found him. And in the basement of his mother's house, in which he lived, we found quite an assortment of things. Underwear, makeup, cosmetics. Photos," she said meaningfully. "Items which he'd stolen from his victims' homes weeks before each of their deaths." She was silent for a moment. "If only the women had realized what was happening when they missed personal items . . . a pair of underwear . . . a tube of lipstick."

"Or photos," I added, a shiver walking across the back of my neck.

"Or photos."

I took a deep breath. "So these guys steal underwear, cosmetics, photos and so on, and do what with them?"

"Fantasize. Imagine. Wear the underwear, use the makeup, smell the perfume, look at the photos. And, usually, masturbate. What you have to realize is that most of these men don't know much about women at all. From adolescence, they have been unable to sustain successful relationships. Women are alien beings to them." She paused. "These are the men we call the 'organized killers.' These are not the perpetrators of the spontaneous sexual homicides. These men commit planned and organized murders. At the crime scenes, everything speaks of control — control taken to extremes. The motivations for the killings are most likely sexual, but they're deep-seated drives, not the sorts that can be satisfied by merely abducting a woman, killing her and having sex with her body. That's too primitive for them. No, these men are much more complicated than that. What they do to a woman, they do *before* she's dead. The sadism is an important part of it. They want their victims to feel pain and they want them to know that they feel it and that it pleases them."

She fell silent. For my part, I had nothing to say. The implications of what she had just told me were too horrible to permit my mind to function logically.

"My work," she continued, "consisted of developing a methodology to identify and flag certain behaviors in juvenile offenders. I identified these behaviors from the files of dozens of serial killers and from interviews with them. After I'd interviewed, oh, about twenty serial killers, and the same sorts of juvenile incidents kept cropping up again and again, the realization came to me that I ought to take this information and apply it somehow. It could be used as a predictor of possible future criminal behavior, I thought. It could serve as a huge red flag for law enforcement agencies and could go with these individuals' files."

"Seems logical," I said.

She smiled. "I'd barely begun my work — I was three or four years into it, and I'd only identified and interviewed about twenty juveniles, when this happened." She passed the fingers of one hand over her eyes. "Anyhow, to conclude this rather rambling discourse, when Sandy told me about your photo-sending burglar, I was interested in the case for two reasons. One, it has the hallmarks of a fetish burglary and it seemed to me that you'd been given a chance to throw a wrench into this man's fantasy. Interrupt it before it goes much farther."

"And two?"

She was quiet for a long time. "Two is . . . private."

"Private?"

"Yes."

I felt rebuffed and more than a little irritated. "Okay."

I guess I wasn't able to keep my emotions out of my voice because Eliane said, "Ah, I've offended you."

"By not telling me your private reason? Hardly. You don't have to tell me anything about yourself."

"However, I sense some . . . irritation. Or is it skepticism?"

I sighed. "No, not exactly skepticism. But this fetish burglary thing . . . it's so extreme. You may well be right, but I can hardly rule out the other two possibilities without giving them due consideration. My clients deserve that from me."

"You're wasting your time, you know," she said bluntly.

"That remains to be seen," I told her frostily. "Right now I don't know enough to rule anything out."

"As you wish," Eliane said. She rose abruptly. "I have work to do, Miss Reece. As, I imagine, do you."

Amazed, I realized the interview was over. I was being thrown out because I didn't agree with her.

"Come," she said, "I'll show you to the door." She made her way around the sofa. "Let me take your arm," she said, holding out a hand to me. "It's less awkward that way."

I walked to her side and she reached for me, sliding a hand down my arm to my hand, then tucking it companionably under hers, leading me across the broad expanse of carpet. I was silent, once again acutely aware of her scent and her nearness, and I felt suddenly annoyed at my own response. What was going on? I wasn't a sex-starved spinster. Besides, I was more than a little angry with this woman for being so pig-headed. How could I be vulnerable to stirrings of the libido when I was steaming mad?

"You're uncomfortable," she observed, pausing in the doorway. "What is it? Does my blindness upset you?"

Her blindness was the least of the things about her that upset me and I laughed aloud at the very thought. "No, not at all."

"Well, what then?"

"I . . ." It was on the tip of my tongue to just

blurt it right out, to tell the truth. *What disturbs me? You. You disturb me. You. Eliane. From the instant I saw you, a part of me began to resonate to you like a plucked string.* That's what I wanted to say. That and the fact that I thought her a stubborn, spoiled, narrow-minded fanatic. Instead, I decided to tell something akin to the truth, but not too far removed from it. "Maybe it's the subject matter," I told her. "Monsters. What you said earlier made me realize that I have a special place in my memory where I've been stuffing my monsters. A black hole."

"Ah," she said. "I thought as much." She patted my arm. "Perhaps we can trade stories someday."

"I'd like that," I replied, realizing this was only *pro forma* politeness on her part. The chances of our sitting around over beer and pizza trading stories were about as remote as my taking tea with Catherine Deneuve.

"Here we are," she said, having indeed walked me to the front door. "Do you have a coat?"

"Yeah. It's here." I found my bomber jacket on the coat rack and shrugged into it.

She opened the door for me and held out her hand. "Very nice to have met you," she said. "Good luck with your case."

I took her hand in mine, shook it, uttered some nicety, and, feeling dismissed, hurried away down the wide stone walk to my car. By the time I reached the end of Oceanside Avenue I was, unaccountably, weeping. I rounded the corner onto the highway and once I figured I was out of earshot of the house, I laid rubber savagely. An adolescent response, but right at that moment I felt like an adolescent — hot and bothered, rebuffed, and pissed off.

Feeling angry and depressed, I decided to treat myself to the rock cod special at British Fish 'N Chips then go on home and tipple some Glenlivet and brood to music. But as I wheeled up in front of the restaurant I spotted the orange and white CLOSED sign in the window and cursed. It was Monday. Of course. The restaurant was closed on Mondays. *Why not?* I inquired of the gods as I cruised dispiritedly home, hungry, dejected, and irritated with the world.

The message light was flashing on my answering machine when I walked in, but I decided to ignore it. Splashing two fingers of Glenlivet into a glass, I dialed the corner pizza joint, heaved my jacket in the general direction of the coat tree, and piled a few logs on the fireplace grate. Arranging some crumpled newspapers under the logs, and tossing a couple of matches at the whole combustible mess, I popped a tape into my cassette player and sat back, swirling the honey-colored Scotch, letting Joni Mitchell's song, "A Case of You," carry me off. When she came to the part about being a woman of heart and mind, I snorted. That was me, all right. Too much heart and too little mind. A romantic fool, one of my past lovers had called me. Well, I supposed I was.

Another verse of the song — the one about the lonely painter who lived in a box of paints, afraid of the devil, and attracted to people who weren't afraid — seemed meant just for me, too.

Was that it? Did I fear the men I chose to confront? Did I confront them because I feared them? Was I using my clients as some sort of dowsing stick to lead me to monsters, to the things that I feared most? And was that why I was drawn to Eliane — because I sensed in her something that was lacking in myself, an essential courage? I swallowed the rest of my Scotch and got up to pour another when the doorbell rang. My pizza. I tipped the teenage delivery girl a buck and took the pizza into the kitchen where, just to prove I wasn't as far gone as I suspected I was, I extricated two slices from the cardboard carton and put them on a real plate. Paper napkins in hand, I returned to the couch, my Scotch, and my brooding. And the brown envelope of photos.

Carefully, I emptied them out onto the coffee table. There were four, all five inches by eight inches. The first, as Liz had already told me, was of Laura's head. Clearly her graduation picture, it had been cropped from her torso and superimposed on a background of blue sky with clouds where it floated, disembodied. I had to admit, it was pretty creepy. I looked closely. The cropping was a good job.

The next photo combined Laura's head with that of a woman's bare-breasted torso. Having never seen Laura's breasts, I couldn't say if this was her or not. I'd have to take Liz's word that it was. I fetched my magnifying glass from my desk in the back bedroom and examined the second photo closely. It looked fuzzy and grainy — obviously the result of being enlarged. But someone had worked hard. The head and the torso seemed in perfect proportion. They too, floated in cloudy blue space. Weird.

The third photo was of the head and torso plus one arm. A right arm. The arm was bare and had been joined to the torso very expertly. But the curious thing about it was that it was raised, palm outward, as if warning or begging or pleading.

The fourth photo added, as I expected, the left arm. Or at least part of it — shoulder to elbow. The rest of the arm disappeared behind the torso. Were we to understand that the arm was voluntarily tucked behind the back? Or was it tied there? I studied the position of the arm. It was impossible to tell. But I guessed that was what the sender wanted — speculation. He was sending someone (Laura? Liz?) a message, and it was up to her to figure it out.

I tossed the photos onto the coffee table. My young friend Lester Baines might be able to tell me something about how the photos had been put together and maybe, just maybe, track down the lab that had done them. Because this wasn't a home darkroom job. Anyone can develop black and white photos — I did it as a kid in my parents' bathroom. But color prints take a whole lot of expensive equipment.

I looked at the photos again and shivered. Such a lot of trouble. But what in hell was the sender saying?

The phone rang, interrupting Joni, and I let my machine take the call. To hell with it. I just didn't feel like talking to anyone tonight. But when it rang again, I began to get worried. Maybe Tonia was calling from Boston. Or perhaps Francis had some information for me. Shit. It seemed that I didn't have the luxury to sit on the couch and spend an evening brooding. Duty called. Feeling aggrieved, I got up to play back my messages. There were three and to my enormous surprise, they were all from Eliane.

"Miss Reece," the last one said, "please return my call. I have something rather . . . urgent to tell you."

I swallowed my Scotch in one gulp and dialed the number she'd left me.

"St. Cyr," answered a well-modulated voice I recognized as Eliane's.

"Caitlin Reece," I responded, trying to ignore my accelerating heartbeat.

"Yes, Miss Reece. Thank you for returning my call. I want to explain something," she said after a short pause. "I was rather short with you this afternoon. In fact, I . . . dismissed you. I feel I owe you an explanation."

My spirits lifted a little. Perhaps her coolness hadn't been due to a personal grooming problem on my part after all. "Yes?" I replied.

"I needed time to think," Eliane said. "Also, I needed Romany to check my files. I needed to be sure." I could hear her exhale. "You see, your case, this photograph thing, well, it touched a nerve with me. I told you that I was involved with a case similar to yours several years ago. That wasn't the whole truth. The truth is, I was involved with a case that sounds exactly like yours. The similarity

. . . unnerved me. And so I dismissed you. I apologize for that." She paused, evidently waiting for my reply.

"I accept your apology," I said awkwardly, realizing something of the sort was expected of me. With a stab of disappointment, I realized, too, that she was lying. Or at least not telling me the complete truth.

"I wondered, well, that is . . ." she trailed off, and I waited, mystified. "I'd like to hire you," she said finally.

"The *modus operandi* of your case and mine are too similar to be unrelated. I want to know how they are related. I . . . need to know it. I need to know if the same perpetrator is involved." I could hear her take a deep breath. "And if the two perpetrators turn out to be the same individual — and I can't think how it could be otherwise — I want a few moments alone with him. Because you see this man, the man who is sending the photos, is the man who blinded me. In a prison interview room. He struck me across the side of the head with his shackled hands. His grinning face was the last thing I ever saw."

"Theo Blalock?" I asked, my voice hoarse. "Laura's husband? He did that to you?"

"No, not Theo Blalock. The name he used then was Martin Fell. Obviously he's changed names."

I thought for a moment, trying to find some reason to refuse her. Mistaking my silence, she upped the ante: "I'll open my files to you," she said. "You can have access to everything I knew about Fell as a juvenile. With that information, you'll surely be able to find him. And to build a case against him. I'll even assist you," she added.

I groaned silently. It was certainly tempting. "Let me think about it," I equivocated. "I'm pretty tired right now. I want to sleep on it — you know, see how I feel in the morning. I need to be sure there's no conflict with the work I'm doing for Liz and Laura."

"I don't see —" she started to say, and then broke off. "All right. Until tomorrow, then."

"Tomorrow."

I hung up the phone very carefully, then sat back down on the couch, staring at nothing in particular. Finally I felt a bump against my leg and, looking down, recognized the familiar bulk of Repo, my portly gray cat.

"Frrrrr?" he asked. "Mmmmfrrrr?"

"I don't know," I told him. "But let's play Scarlett O'Hara again — one of my role models. Let's think about all this tomorrow."

But of course my perverse subconscious wouldn't cooperate. Chewing on the matter like a dog worrying a bone, it woke me at just after three. I tossed and turned, fluffed the pillow, rearranged the cats, had a few sips of water, but nothing helped.

"Okay, okay," I groused, sitting up in bed and turning on the bedside light.

Repo moaned and covered his eyes with one paw. Jeoffrey, who was blind anyhow, snored on.

"Do I want to work for Eliane?" I asked Repo. "That seems to be the question of the hour."

"Snorffff," he said.

"Yeah, I know. I already have a client. I have other concerns, though. What are they? Nice of you to ask. Well, what I'm mainly concerned about, apart from the fact that she's not telling me the whole truth, is that Eliane may have Froot Loops for brains. I'm sure that at one time she was a crackerjack in her field, but I think the years may have addled her. How does she know that her guy and mine are one and the same? She has absolutely nothing to go on. Did she consult her crystal ball, or what? Heck, why assume that Theo's guilty of *anything* let alone being this monster who clobbered her? And God, she's so damned *pushy*. Like her opinion is holy writ. There might well be other reasons for Laura's receiving the photos." I ticked them off on my fingers. "One, extortion. Someone may be setting up Laura, or Liz, to squeeze money out of them. Two, yeah, it might be hubby trying to scare Laura back to his arms, just like Liz thinks. Three, it might be something else."

"Ffffrrrrttt?"

"What something else? I don't know yet. And I really won't be able to even hazard a guess until I get a little further into this. But y'know what? Answers always suggest themselves. Yep. The more you get to know about the players in the game, the greater the possibilities. And frankly, Eliane's theory is at the bottom of my list."

"Mmmmmmnorr. Ffffnorrr."

"Right. Explore all possibilities. Leave no stone unturned. I quite agree."

"Snorrfff."

"Ah yes, there is that. The undeniable attraction

of working for the sexy and aristocratic Ms. St. Cyr. Oops — Dr. St. Cyr. She certainly stirred up my hormones. But ye gods, aren't I a little old for those shenanigans? Can you see us pawing and snorting on the fifteen-thousand-dollar Oriental carpet? I don't think so. Jeez. Besides, she'd be a *client*." I prodded Repo with one foot. "Very unprofessional. Nope, I think I'll just plod along myself. That's what we gumshoes do best, right?" Only heavy feline breathing answered me. So, the stirrings of the subconscious apparently satisfied, I fell asleep.

TUESDAY

Chapter 7

As I measured scoops of coffee into my Krups' filter basket the next morning, starving cats twining 'round my ankles, I put in a call to Liz. Just in case. But, as I had been willing to bet, the wandering Laura had not returned. Liz sounded just this side of hysterical.

"Oh for heaven's sake, go mow your lawns," I told her, interrupting another episode of wailing. During the night a rather interesting theory had taken shape in my mind, and while it was far too soon to discuss it with Liz, I needed to help her out a little. Give her some hope. "I'm working on something," I told her evasively. "Try not to worry too much. I'll be in touch later." Then I hung up. Before she had a chance to quiz me about details which were admittedly sketchy.

"And you guys chill out," I told the cats as their moans escalated to fever pitch. Dividing a can of Tender Turkey into thirds, I plunked the dishes on the cat mat, turned on the Krups and ran to pull on my clothes. It was barely five-thirty, but I hoped that playing the early bird would allow me to catch up with a certain employee of the Pan Pacific Cannery. Preferably before he left for work. Pouring a cup of coffee and grabbing my bomber jacket, I hurried out into the pre-dawn chill.

Theo Blalock's apartment was one of a quartet of buff-colored stucco duplexes in James Bay, close to the ocean, but too close to downtown to be a really good address. These were rental properties, distinguished by a lack of flower beds and attention paid to lawns. By the feeble orange glow of the streetlights, I found 17-A Arbutus and parked across the street where I had a good view of the front door. Laura had listed a black Cherokee as Blalock's car and lo and behold, a dusty black Cherokee sat in front of 17-A, waiting for its owner to emerge. I hunkered down in my seat, sipping coffee and thinking. As I had thought yesterday when I tracked Blalock to the cannery, this was far too easy. It was almost as if . . . as if no one ever dreamed someone would come looking for him. Hmmm. Who could have been so short-sighted? Or arrogant. Were Laura and Blalock in some scheme together? It sure looked that way. A scheme which my hiring had derailed. I was willing to bet that was the reason for Laura's abrupt disappearance. She knew better than to hang around: sooner or later, I'd catch up with her. Well, she had a surprise coming. I intended to catch up with her anyhow. And when I did, I intended to shake her 'til her teeth rattled for scaring Liz half to death. And for probably breaking Liz's heart. But right now, I wanted that little shit Blalock, presumably the mastermind of this sorry scheme.

As if on cue, the door of 17-A opened and a thin young dark-haired guy dressed in jeans and a blue and gray varsity jacket stepped out onto the sidewalk. Zipping his jacket, he walked over to the Cherokee, fished in his pocket for keys . . . and I fell in behind him.

"Theo Blalock?" I asked.

He didn't respond.

Puzzled, I raised my voice. "Blalock — turn around!"

He did. Under the sickly orange sodium vapor light I saw a pasty, thin-faced kid of about twenty-five, with longish dark hair combed back off a high forehead and cruel, avid eyes. He looked at me and smiled a goblin's smile, full of dreadful secrets, and I thought suddenly, *Eliane's right. My God, but she's right.* Then someone hit me from behind with something large that contacted my head with the sound a cantaloupe might make when you drop it on the kitchen floor. I saw constellations of pinwheels, galaxies of sunbursts, and then I saw nothing at all.

* * * * *

"How many fingers?" asked someone in white with a stethoscope dangling from his neck.

"Aaaaagh," I managed to answer, struggling up from the depths of some black pit.

"Concussion," he said over his shoulder. "Let's get her loaded. Check her wallet. See who we're to call."

"Aaaaagh," I said again, but an oxygen mask clamped itself to my nose and mouth like the obscene kiss of some phantasmagorical beast and I gave up. My head felt about the size of the Goodyear blimp and there was a horrible clanging noise deep inside it. The pit out of which I had crawled seemed particularly inviting so I let myself topple back over the edge in a slow-motion fall into inky oblivion.

WEDNESDAY

Chapter 8

I came around with the worst headache I could remember but, alas, no recollection of the terrific party that must have preceded it. I opened my eyes to gloom. What was this dim place — someone's bedroom? But whose? For the life of me, I couldn't remember. Huh. Some party. I tried to move toes and fingers, found I could, then tentatively attempted to sit up. No good. I got as far as raising my head off the pillow when a horrible nausea overtook me. Turning my head, I retched, but nothing came up. Shaky, sick, I subsided.

"Water," someone said and held a straw to my lips. I slurped. Nothing had ever tasted so good.

"Where am I?" I managed to croak.

"In the hospital. Where head injury patients belong," a calm female voice replied.

The hospital? Which hospital? University Hospital in Toronto, I supposed. The wheels turned slowly in my brain and I recalled with great effort that no, I no longer lived in Toronto. That threw me into a panic because for the life of me, I couldn't recall where I *did* live. Try harder, fool, I told myself. Okay. I (whoever *I* was) had left Toronto for . . . where? I closed my eyes. The west coast. Victoria. I lived in Victoria. I could even conjure up a picture of my house — a black and white Tudor duplex on an oak-lined street with lush green lawns and carefully tended flowerbeds. Got it.

But who the hell was I? Maybe the voice in the room with me had a clue. I decided to be cagey about this, however. For all I knew, one false step meant the rubber room.

"Hey, there," I asked the voice, "who are you?"

"Gray, she doesn't know us," a little girl's voice whispered and for a horrible instant I thought this might be *my* child. Oh my God — had I produced it in a fit of absentmindedness?

"She will," the adult's voice replied.

Then things started to click. Gray. Didn't I know someone named Gray? Yes, indeed. Gray who liked animals. Gray who had been fired from her job as a veterinary assistant for being a "damned Asian witch." Or did I just make that up? Who knew? Gray Ng. That was her name. Animal psychologist and Vietnamese expatriate Gray Ng. But what about the kid? I gave up.

"C'mere, you two," I rasped.

They did. A small Asian woman of indeterminate age, jet black hair cropped short, eyes like anthracite. A skinny girl of obvious Canadian Indian heritage, about ten, black hair neatly braided, narrow clever face, hazel eyes, a gap between her front teeth. I summoned up the name. Jory.

"Caitlin," the kid said. "Are you going to be all right?"

Bingo! Caitlin. Of course. Caitlin Reece. Me. Intrepid private investigator, righter of wrongs, protector of the downtrodden, bulwark of the disenfranchised, champion of the have-nots. The idiot who'd let herself be clobbered from behind by a bad guy. When? This morning?

"Sure," I said with a lot more conviction that I felt. "What day is it?"

Jory looked at Gray then back at me. "Wednesday."

Wednesday? What the hell had happened to Tuesday? Panic seized me. Weren't there places I had to be, people I had to call, things I had to do? Surely there were, but for the life of me I couldn't remember what they might be.

Gray placed a hand on my forehead. "Just rest. You can go home later if you feel up to it. The doctors have said so."

Home. The black and white Tudor duplex. That seemed attractive. But thinking about home made me feel . . . uneasy. Wasn't there some responsibility I had left unmet?

"We have been to your home," Gray said. "We fed the cats."

Oh. Good. But I wonder if they found Pansy. She hides out in the pantry. They might not know.

"We found everyone," Gray said, reading my mind. "Repo made certain we knew where Pansy was. He is most chivalrous."

Good old Repo, I thought, realizing that Gray had just read my mind and I didn't think it at all odd. Well, what the hell. Wasn't that what witches did? No wonder her animal psychology practice was thriving. *I think I'll just rest a while,* I thought. *I feel kinda . . . washed out. All this remembering.*

"Yes. Rest," Gray agreed.

I closed my eyes.

When I opened them again, night had fallen. At least I thought night had fallen. A lamp beside my bed cast a small pool of warm yellow light and beyond its glow I could see the dark shapes I took to be Gray and Jory. Waiting, I guessed. I had to admit it, I was touched.

"Hi, guys," I said. "Whattya say we blow this joint?"

"Brave words," Gray told me, coming to sit on my bed. "But perhaps you ought to see if you can sit up first."

"Sure," I said, demonstrating that indeed I could sit up. In fact, I didn't feel too bad at all. Gray moved out of the way and I dangled both legs over the side of the bed, then stood. No problem. My head hurt, but other than that, I had no complaints. "Where are my clothes?"

"In the closet, Caitlin." Gray turned to Jory. "Jory, go and inform the nursing supervisor that

Miss Reece wishes to check out. Have her locate the proper forms."

Giving me a concerned look, Jory went.

"Thanks," I told Gray as I pulled my jeans on, tossed my hospital gown aside and tugged my T-shirt and pullover over my head. I sat on the edge of the bed and brought my feet up to my hands for shoe-and-sock donning, thinking it wise not to tempt the gods by bending over. Frankly, I was afraid the back of my head might blow out.

"Jory has told me that she wants to come and stay with you when you are released," Gray told me.

I paused in mid-lacing of my Reebok. "What? Why?"

"To take care of you."

I glowered at Gray. "No way. I can take care of myself."

"Evidently."

"No sarcasm here, please."

"I did not intend sarcasm. But surely you realize that in your condition you could use some assistance."

I sat down heavily on the bed. "Yeah. Maybe a little. But I don't want Jory around."

"Then you must tell her that. Her feelings will be hurt."

"Wait a minute. I don't want her around because I'm in the middle of a case. A case which just got very ugly," I said, running a hand over the truffle-sized lump on the back of my head. "To hell with her feelings. It's her safety I'm thinking about."

"Ah," Gray replied.

"What *did* happen to you?" Jory asked, coming back into the room.

"I got careless. A bad guy clobbered me."

She leaned against the wall, silent, waiting, a trick she had learned from Gray.

"Look, I'm happy, flattered even, that the two of you are concerned about me, but I can't have anyone staying with me. There's something . . . screwy about this case. I don't want anyone else involved. Things may get a lot messier before they're resolved."

"Okay," Jory said. "I accept that you might not want to have a kid around. So pick someone bigger."

I goggled at her. "Wait a minute, short stuff—"

"She is correct," Gray interrupted. "A child might not be able to contend with someone who intends you ill. So you must have an adult stay with you for a few days. Otherwise, according to your doctor, you ought to remain here. I am certain you do not want to even consider remaining here. So who do you suggest?"

"What? I don't need a nursemaid, someone following me around, getting in my way, interfering with my business."

"Be sensible," Gray said softly. "You can do as you please—no one will force you to take care of yourself. But be sure you are refusing help for the right reason."

I thought hard, but no right reason suggested itself to me. "Oh all right," I sighed. "Lester. He'll think it's an adventure."

"Ah yes. Lester," Gray said, smiling. "A good choice."

I snorted. "My list of candidates wasn't exactly

long. Let me call him," I said. "Just to be sure. Then I'll sign out and we'll blow this joint."

Lester met us at my place, cheerful and upbeat, though it was the middle of the night. I noticed that my MG was parked in the driveway and decided against asking who drove it home. I was afraid to learn that Gray had teleported it or, worse yet, that Jory had driven the MG while Gray trailed along in her van. Neither piece of information was one I wanted to acquire. That it was there, presumably possessing all its hubcaps and chrome, was good enough for me. While Jory took Lester's overnight bag into the guest bedroom, I laid out the ground rules for him.

"No fussing. No questions. No admonitions."

He nodded, adjusting his aviator glasses nervously.

"Two nights max. And you go off to that camera shop of yours during the day. I have things to do. Places to go. Folks to see. Necks to wring."

Lester and Gray exchanged glances.

"Now what?" I demanded.

"Your vision," Gray replied. "The doctor is afraid you may have attacks of dizziness or double vision. He advises against driving."

"Why didn't *he* tell me all this?" I demanded.

"Because you insisted on signing yourself out," Gray said matter-of-factly.

"Are you sure all this isn't just retaliation for my

making you sit in the back seat last year when *you* were clobbered over the head by a bad guy?"

Gray said nothing.

"Oh, all right." I capitulated. What else could I do? "Why don't we call it a night. I'm sure we all have work to do tomorrow. I know I do."

"You won't forget, will you?" Jory asked me on her way out.

"Forget what?"

She looked at me darkly. "My piano recital. It's on Saturday. At the conservatory."

"Of course not," I told her breezily. "I'll be there. Four o'clock, right?"

"Caitlinnnn, it's *three* o'clock!"

"Just teasing," I fibbed, bending to hug her. "Take care of yourself."

As Gray and Jory walked off into the night, I called after them, "Hey, thanks for coming to the hospital. I appreciate it."

"Our pleasure," Gray replied.

That left Lester and me alone together.

"It's past your bedtime, kiddo," I told him, as he stood indecisively in the hall, hands in the pockets of his khaki pants.

"Er, well, I just wanted to say, that is, I've asked Doris to look after the shop, and —"

"We can talk about it tomorrow," I told him. "If you want to play chauffeur so badly, I might just let you do it. Wait right there." I fetched the brown envelope of photos from the living room coffee table and tossed it at him. "Study these."

"Okay," he said, unable to disguise the excitement in his voice. "Okay." Then he disappeared into the spare bedroom where, a few moments later, I heard him whistling. I shook my head. So easily pleased.

And that left me alone with myself.

I poured myself a finger of Scotch and carried it into the my bedroom. Repo and Jeoffrey were already curled together at the end of the bed and I sat down in the old maple rocker in the corner, watching them sleep and thinking how glad I was to be home. And how lucky I was to have such friends. Closing my eyes, I rocked a little. The cats snored. I sipped my Scotch, sighing, and suddenly . . . the world shifted and I was somewhere else. Someplace dark. Someplace vast. Someplace that echoed. I smelled the sea, touched walls that were hard and crusty, felt water around my ankles, tasted blood in my mouth. I wanted to run away, but somewhere up ahead there was something that I needed more than I needed to flee, something that drove me on. But up ahead, too, was a huge, menacing presence, a terrifying *thing*. Terror wrapped me in its black wings, folding me close, suffocating me . . .

I dropped my glass on the floor and came awake with a start, the tag-end of a dream disappearing from my mind like morning mist. Yawning, I stripped off my clothes and tossed them in the corner. As I wrapped myself in my sheets, I had the vague feeling that the dream I had just woken from was one I definitely did not want to tune into again. But before I had a chance to worry more about it, I slid into sleep.

THURSDAY

Chapter 9

Even though I'd slept for most of two days, I awoke feeling flannelly of tongue, fragile of pate (understandably), and shaky of limb. Nothing that a strong cup of coffee and breakfast at British Fish 'N Chips couldn't fix, I decided. A shower helped things, but halfway through my ablutions, I realized that I had become afflicted with what I decided I was going to call Fugue Drift. Without warning, I just kinda zoned out and three, four, eleven minutes later, I came back to earth wondering where in hell I had been. This happened to me once in the shower, twice when I was looking for clean socks, and again as I was searching for a coffee filter.

"Lester!" I yelled when I had my wits about me and coffee perking. "Front and center!"

"Coming!" he called, and joined me in a moment, tucking the tail of a blue chambray shirt into clean jeans.

I studied him. A little taller than me, sandy hair, friendly blue eyes behind aviator glasses, a Pepsodent smile, he looked exactly what he was — a helluva nice guy.

"Who irons your shirts for you?" I asked.

"Huh?"

"Your shirts. I want to hire whoever irons your shirts."

"Oh, er, well, I do."

"Give me strength." I rolled my eyes. "The deal's off. Listen up. Here's the day's agenda. One, breakfast at British Fish 'N Chips." Was it my imagination, or did he turn pale at the prospect? What was wrong with rock cod for breakfast? "Two, a return to the scene of the crime. I still want to talk to Theo Blalock."

"Who?"

Oh yeah. I'd forgotten — Lester didn't know anything about my case. Well, I'd have to fill him in on the details I wanted him to know as we drove to breakfast. "A guy. Then, three, depending on what we find at two, we might have to drive to Esquimalt. Or, four, that arts magnet school. Then we'll have lunch somewhere. That seem okay to you?"

"Sure," he said enthusiastically. I sighed. Lester was such a romantic. He assumed the life of a private investigator was glamorous and exciting when mostly it consisted of pretty boring routine work. Unless, of course, you classify getting clobbered by bad guys in the wee hours of the morning to be exciting. I don't. I consider that to be stupid. And I now had another addition to my Most Wanted list: Theo Blalock or Martin Fell or whoever he was calling himself now.

"C'mon then," I told him. "Onward to British Fish 'N Chips."

Lester eyed the Rock Cod Special with little enthusiasm. The tea and toast he'd ordered arrived just after my fish and he brightened a little at that. At this hour we were the establishment's only patrons.

"That won't hold you 'til ten o'clock, let alone noon," I told him. "You need protein. How do you think you're gonna grow up and be a private eye if you don't eat right?" I punctuated my phrases by waving a fat French fry dunked in cole slaw sauce at him.

"Er, I don't know," he said, sounding sorry. Or maybe he sounded ill. I wasn't sure.

"Hmmph. Tea and toast indeed."

He poured himself a second cup of tea. "So we're off to the place you got clobbered?"

I slitted my eyes at him. "Careful, junior. But to answer your question, yes. Seventeen-A Arbutus Street. James Bay. Home of a certain Theo Blalock. Husband — oops, ex-husband — of one of my clients. To fill you in on the details of this sorry mess so far, I was hired to try and determine who is sending my client the photos I gave you last night and to make him stop."

Lester nodded, listening intently. At any moment I expected him to take notes.

"The wife insisted the husband has nothing to do with this, so in an effort to rule him — Theo Blalock — out, I visited his place of employment, missed him, and decided to visit him at his home Tuesday morning. I was standing talking to him when I was, as you so colloquially put it, clobbered."

Lester had the good grace to blush. "But not by Blalock."

"No, Sherlock, not by Blalock."

"The wife?" he guessed.

"Maybe. But why is just as interesting to me as who."

"Someone didn't want you talking to him."

"Evidently. One wonders what they're afraid of."

"And how they knew you were you."

"Run that one by me again?"

"Well, how did whoever clobbered you know that you were Caitlin Reece and not, oh, the lady across the street or the meter reader or —"

"Got it," I interrupted him. "It's looking more and more like the wife is involved. She's the only one of the pair who knows me." I drummed my fingers on the tabletop. "You're pretty smart for a shopkeeper."

He fought a smile.

I dug some bills out of my pocket. "Time to play chauffeur."

* * * * *

Seventeen-A Arbutus looked sleazier at nine-thirty than it had at five-thirty. Daylight can be so unkind. By the light of the feeble sun, I could see one lone clump of daffodils proclaiming spring to the hapless inhabitants of number seventeen. Grim. Lester parked his Samurai in the spot the Cherokee had occupied that fateful morning and we got out and stood on the sidewalk, both of us blinking in a pale March sunshine that threw no shadows.

"Um, what do you want me to do?" he asked.

"Watch my back. If anyone with a large, blunt instrument appears, yell."

He stood a little taller. "Okay."

I walked to the peeling, dark brown door of A, Lester on my heels, and knocked. Nothing. Sighing, I knocked again.

"Znot there," a voice called from behind me.

A skinny little dark-complexioned boy, wearing patched jeans and a mud-colored sweater that should have belonged to his little brother, crouched on the grass, some indefinable toy in his hand. He wore sneakers, but no socks.

"Hi there," Lester said cheerfully.

"Znot there," the little boy repeated, running the wheels of his toy across the dead grass.

"Does a man named Theo live here?" Lester asked.

The urchin shook his head, wiping a dirty nose with an equally dirty finger.

"Where's he gone?" Lester said, kneeling down beside him. "Gone to work?"

"Gone 'way," the kid said mournfully. Then, striking Lester in the knee with his plastic truck, he said "Harrrummm. RRRRRummmm. See weenie."

"Jesus," I muttered. "You two boys can stay here and discuss anatomical parts. I'll find the landlord. Maybe Blalock really has flown the coop."

The landlord turned out to be a harried-looking Pakistani woman of about thirty, skinny, dressed in clean faded jeans and a surprisingly white sweatshirt. "Theo Blalock?" She laughed. "You're too late. He moved yesterday. While I was in court getting an eviction order for him. He skipped out on three months' rent."

"Darn!" I exclaimed. "He owes me money, too."

The landlord shrugged. "Tough luck."

"I don't suppose you know where he might have gone?"

She laughed again. "No. These laboring types come and go. Although Blalock lasted longer than most. Almost a year. He works at the cannery across the bridge. At least he did. They might know something there."

"Thanks. Oh, by the way," I asked, thinking of the guy who had answered Theo's phone on Monday, "did his roommate share the apartment with him the whole time he was here?"

She looked blank. "Roommate?" Evidently this was news to her. "As far as I knew, he lived here by himself. What makes you think he had a roommate?"

"I called here once, pretty early in the morning, and another guy answered."

Her eyebrows made twin peaks, then she shook her head. "I don't know who that could be."

We were silent, the two sorry Stiffed-By-Theo

Sisters. Then she said, "Say, if you find out where he went, you know, anything like that, well, my name is Renata Sethi. I'm in the book."

"I'll let you know," I told her.

"Thanks. Ajay really liked him. He's very sad." I decided not to ask who the grieving Ajay might be. Her parrot, for all I knew. Mistaking my silence for commiseration, she offered, "Hey, he left a couple boxes of junk. You can have 'em if you want. Maybe you can sell the stuff, collect some of what he owes you."

I was going to refuse, but then I thought, why not? Sifting through Blalock's junk would be a great job for Lester. He might even unearth A Clue. "I'll send my . . . brother," I told her.

Lester and the urchin were still deep in conversation. "Go see the landlord. She's in G. Blalock's gone but he left a couple boxes of stuff. It might be worthwhile looking through."

While Lester hustled off to G, I regarded the kid. The landlord's son, I decided. Under the dirt, there was a family resemblance. This must be the doleful Ajay. "Rrrrummm," the kid said hopefully, holding the toy up for my inspection. "See weenie."

Damned if he didn't have a one-track mind. "Listen, I'd keep it in my pants if I were you," I suggested.

"Tio see weenie," he said mournfully. Jesus. What was he anyhow — a junior flasher? Fortunately Lester appeared at just that moment, hidden behind an armful of boxes.

"C'mon," I told him, opening the Samurai's back

flap so he could dump the stuff in. "I'm growing weary of Ajay's confessions about his weenie. The kid clearly has a problem."

"Oh?" Lester said with interest, dumping the boxes inside.

"Forget it," I told him. "We have other fish to fry. Let's split. We're a day too late. Apparently Mr. Blalock moved rather suddenly. Yesterday, in fact. While I was flat on my back in Jubilee Hospital." I ground my teeth in frustration.

"I guess he's really, well, afraid of you," Lester said admiringly. We both climbed into the Samurai.

"I guess. Makes you wonder why, though, doesn't it?"

"It's obvious, isn't it?" Lester asked, adjusting his glasses and turning to look at me. "Or am I missing something? It's just like your client Liz thought — this photo thing is Blalock's doing. He's trying to scare Laura back to him."

"Nah. I don't think so."

"Well, what then?"

"Damned if I know. I'd say extortion. Except for one thing."

"What's that?"

"Well, if Laura and Theo cooked this up between them, then she knew full well that he was going to send the photos to drive Liz into a frenzy. Seeing the photos wouldn't have fazed her a bit. But she just about lost it when she discovered them in Liz's truck. Hell, she was a basket case when I went to collect her from her friend's place on Sunday night. She's scared to death and I can't figure what of."

"Hmmm," Lester said. "It seems we need to talk to Laura."

"Excuse me?"

"Okay, okay. You need to talk to her. I need to drive. To Willows Arts Magnet School."

"Right. You've got a good memory, kiddo."

"Thanks," he muttered, signaling and pulling into traffic. I could tell that being a chauffeur wouldn't hold him for long.

The same fiftyish, frizzy-haired clerk was at work behind the counter in the administration office of Laura's school. At least I presumed she was at work. She was staring intently at a computer screen, tapping a key now and then. The machine beeped at her occasionally and finally, clearly frustrated, she breathed a *sotto voce* "Fuck!" and sat back, tapping one long cerise nail on her desk. I sympathized with her. Computers were not my forte either.

I cleared my throat.

"Yes?" she inquired testily from her desk, then recognizing me, got up quickly and came to the counter. "You!" she said excitedly, clearly rifling her memory for my name.

"Reece. Caitlin Reece. I'm afraid I didn't catch your name last time," I invented.

"Evans. Becky Evans. You're here about Ms. Neal, right?"

"Right." I lowered my voice to a whisper. "But let's keep it quiet. She may be in a lot of trouble."

She exhaled sharply and I smelled wintergreen gum. "I thought so. All those frantic phone calls. All that time off. Really! The Headmaster is just about to terminate her contract." Her too? Then she could join hubby on the unemployment rolls. Hadn't Pink Sweater at the cannery said the boss was about to fire Theo's ass, too? Seems the estranged duo had a lot to discuss these days.

"Well, maybe you can help her," I suggested.

"Me? How?"

"We need to find her," I said, including her in the action.

She nodded sagely.

"Once we find her, we can protect her."

Another nod.

"From *him,*" I intoned.

"I knew it!" she breathed.

"But she's not at home. Hasn't been for two days."

"Where do you think she might be?"

"A friend's? What about Alana what's-her-name?"

"Miss Cameron? No. She's inquired about Ms. Neal two days in a row. She's very worried. So, no, I don't think she knows anything."

"Is Laura friendly with any of the other teachers?"

"I don't really know. Probably Miss Cameron could tell you that."

This was going nowhere fast. "Listen, I need a favor."

"Well, if I can . . ." she said uncertainly.

"Her personnel file. It might have information in it that would help me find her. You know, next-of-kin, that sort of thing."

"Well, I don't know . . ." she said, her eyes darting to a black filing cabinet in the corner of the office.

"Beck, she needs your help," I said, laying it on

thick. "And I wouldn't take the file far — just to the ladies' room."

She nodded, making up her mind. "Just a minute."

It took her ten seconds to yank open the filing cabinet, retrieve Laura's file, slam the drawer, and hustle back over to me. "The ladies' room is just down the hall to the left," she said helpfully.

"Great!" I told her. "You won't regret this."

In the ladies' john — a two-stall, one-sink cubbyhole which smelled strongly of Lysol — I locked myself in one of the cubicles, sat down, and started to read. Laura Neal (she never had taken her husband's name) had graduated from U Vic in 1988 and had been teaching at Willows for five years. Apart from some summer employment, this was the only job she'd ever had. I wrote down the summer jobs she'd held — as a clerk at Ivy's Bookstore in Oak Bay and bookkeeper for a boatyard out toward Sooke — but they were pretty slim pickings. As next of kin, she'd listed her mom, a Mrs. Alice Neal on Rhododendron Place, in Sooke. That jibed with what her friend Alana had told me. Interestingly enough, she did not list Theo as an emergency contact in case of illness or accident, not even when her file was updated after her marriage last year. Hmmm. Instead, she listed Alana Cameron. They were, it seemed, very good friends. I closed the file folder. Perhaps another visit to Miss Cameron was in order.

I got up, flushed for the sake of appearances, and decided to take a peek at myself in the bathroom mirror. Mistake. I looked pale, pasty, and ill. No roses bloomed in my cheeks today. Even my hair, usually springy and unruly, seemed limp and dispirited. And I'd made the mistake of wearing a forest green wool turtleneck — it made me look bilious. Jeez. All this from a crack on the head? Wincing, I fingered the back of my cranium where Blalock's cohort (who? the demure Laura?) had clobbered me. Goddamn but it hurt. I splashed a little water on my face, dried with a scratchy paper towel, and headed back to the admin office.

Becky was waiting nervously at the counter, tapping a nail on the formica. The look of relief on her face when she saw me and the file was almost comical. She fairly snatched it from me, galloped over to the file cabinet, stuffed it in, and slammed the drawer closed. That done, she smoothed imaginary wrinkles from her skirt and sweater, patted her Brillo pad do, and came back to the counter. I ripped a piece of paper off a scratch pad that lay conveniently close to hand, wrote my home phone number on it, and held it up for Becky. She took it reluctantly, clearly wondering what new breaches of protocol would be expected of her.

"If you hear from Laura, or hear anything about her that you think I should know, please call me," I said. "Call with anything, no matter how trivial you think it might be. If I'm not there, leave the message on my recorder."

She looked up and I was surprised to see genuine concern in her eyes. "She seems so . . . frail," Becky said. "It's hard to believe anyone would want to hurt her. Don't worry. If I hear anything, anything at all, I'll call you."

"Thanks," I told her, and hurried out to rejoin Lester. He had abandoned the Samurai in favor of the same bench on which the Three Lechers had been sitting the last time I visited the school. He, however, had his nose buried in a photography magazine, not a sex rag. I wondered fleetingly just what young Lester did for sex. I presumed he preferred girls but realized that I had never heard him declare an interest in either gender. Hmmm. Oh well, maybe he was just a late bloomer. But who was I to be judgmental, anyhow? My own sex life wasn't exactly the stuff of novels at the moment.

"C'mon, kiddo," I said. "Let's treat ourselves to lunch downtown. Salmon sandwiches and apple crisp at Burt's. Whaddya say?"

"Sounds great."

While Lester drove, I thought. Or tried to. Dammit, the more I thought about this, the more it seemed all roads led to Laura. I was beginning to believe that if I found her, I'd find all the answers. If I could shake them out of her. And that was a big if. I thought back to my one interview with her at Maggie's. She was clearly terrified of something and I was willing to bet it wasn't Theo. I sighed. Something didn't add up here. Closing my eyes, I tried to weave together an explanation for what had been going on. Laura and Theo wanted money. Together they devised a scheme to get it. Laura would represent herself as being on the run from an abusive husband, and take refuge with a vulnerable, well-off dyke. She'd wrap the dyke around one pale finger. Then she'd start receiving unsettling photos in the mail. Photos that would eventually result in an extortion note: "Pay me $5,000 and I'll leave the two of you in peace." Something like that. I frowned. The scenario seemed logical. A good scam. Except for one thing — it hadn't happened that way. As soon as

Laura had seen the photos, she'd bolted. And not even my masterful professional presence could keep her at her job or in that neat little bungalow. She was gone. And Theo, too, was gone. Were they on the run from the same thing? And if so, what? Or who? Clearly, something had gone very wrong. And I didn't think it was just my ferocious self.

I closed my eyes. Lester had the heater cranked up and it was a little too warm in the Samurai. I started to drift off.

. . . under the other-worldly orange light of a streetlamp, a narrow, pale face materialized like some sickly night-blooming flower. Dark hair swept back from a high, clever forehead. Dark, dark eyes blazed. He smiled — a goblin's smile, full of private glee — and cocked his head on one side. He wore a black, scuffed jacket over a dark shirt and pants. With a start, I realized that he was exactly my height. And so slim that I probably outweighed him. But the sense of menace that emanated from him made me want to back up a pace or two to put more air between us. Stubborn, I held my ground.

"Well, you're back," he said. "And here I thought you'd gone away. But no, your kind never does. Well, no matter. I'll get what I want. I will have her." He chuckled. "I've already paid for her, you see."

Then he stepped into a patch of shadows and disappeared.

Hollering, I came awake to find myself in Lester's Samurai.

"Jesus Christ!" I yelled. With my memory of Blalock's face had come flooding back another memory, a memory of the woman who wanted to help me, the woman I had forgotten about until just now, a woman who claimed there were monsters in the world. Eliane St. Cyr.

"What?" Lester swerved so violently that the Samurai veered into the next lane. Fortunately it was empty. "Caitlin, what?"

"Stop! Pull over! Find me a phone!"

Lester swung the wheel and the nimble little car leaped into the left-turn lane. In a jiffy we were wheeling into a gas station, and I wrenched the door open and ran for the phone. My damaged brain cells had somehow yielded up the memory of Eliane's phone number along with her name. God, how could I have just forgotten all about her? I punched her number with no great feeling of hope. What must she think of me? Hadn't I promised to call the next day?

"St. Cyr residence," said a voice I didn't recognize.

"Um, I'd like to speak to Eliane."

"I'm sorry. She's . . . resting," the voice informed me.

"Unless she's receiving the last rites, wake her up," I said, my temper barely in check. "She's not going to thank you for missing this call." Or so I hoped.

"Your name, please?"

"Reece. Caitlin Reece."

And then I waited. The traffic whizzed by on Pandora Street behind me, a few lone seagulls wheeled and squawked overhead, the gas pumps did a land-office business, and I was getting a headache. I had just about decided that the answer would be no, thank you, Miss Reece, Dr. St. Cyr really doesn't want to talk to you, when I heard Eliane's voice.

"Yes, Caitlin?" she asked, her voice neutral.

"I . . . I'd like to come and see you. There are some things I'd like to talk to you about."

"I see," she replied, no great interest in her voice.

Jesus, this was hard. "I didn't call you back because I got knocked in the head by one of Blalock's cronies," I told her. "I guess it addled my brains because I forgot all about phoning you. I spent a day in Jubilee Hospital, in the Twilight Zone. And I'm not certain that I'm not still in it."

"What do you mean?" she asked, concerned now.

"Well, dammit, I was having a snooze just a minute ago and I heard Blalock talking to me. In my head!"

Silence again. Then: "Please come over. I think we should talk."

I felt a vast sense of relief. "Thanks. But there's a problem. I can't drive — the doctor thinks I might see double now and then. And my young friend who's driving me around, well, he'd have to wait for me."

"That's unnecessary. I'll send Sylvie, my driver," she said. "Where are you?"

"We're going to have lunch right now. At Burt's in Trounce Alley. Why don't you have Sylvie meet me, say, at the Inner Harbor in about an hour?"

"Fine," Eliane said. "And Caitlin?"

"Yeah?"

"I'm glad you called."

I wasn't sure if I was, but it was something that needed to be done. If Eliane had information that would help me wrap this case up, I'd better talk to her. Even if she was a fruitcake. "I'll see you soon," I told her.

* * * * *

"Have you ever thought that maybe, you know, maybe you ought to just forget it," Lester said as he dug into his apple crisp.

"Forget what?"

"All of it. Chasing Blalock. And Laura. I mean, Liz hired you to protect Laura from Blalock. But now it looks like Laura's in this thing, too. It may well be you she's afraid of. That might be why she took off. Maybe she doesn't need protection after all." He shrugged.

I shook my head. "No dice. I like answers. I want to know what the hell is going on. I want to know why the photos scared Laura so badly. I want to know what Theo and Laura were fighting about. I want to know why the two of them are on the run — separately or together. And the only folks who can give me those answers are Laura and Blalock. So I have to track them down. Or one of them, at least. Besides," I said, "Liz hired me to find out who was sending the photos and stop them, remember? Not to protect Laura. That's Liz's theory — that Theo's behind things. It's not necessarily mine. Also," I fingered the egg on the back of my head, "this has gotten to be personal."

"Yeah, I figured as much." Lester sighed, then gestured for the waiter to bring us more hot water for tea.

I finished the last of my dessert and sat back, massaging my eyes. I definitely had a headache. I wanted aspirins. Failing that, I wanted to remove my head and put it in a cold place for a while. Maybe Antarctica.

"So how long will you be at this St. Cyr place?"

I shrugged. "No longer than I have to be. She thinks that Blalock is really Martin Fell, a juvie who whacked her over the head eight years ago when she was interviewing him in prison."

Lester raised an eyebrow.

"Yeah, talk about history repeating itself. Anyhow, she has a pretty extensive file on Fell and wants me to take a look at it. It might help to locate him, she thinks."

"Yeah, but it's, what, eight years out of date," Lester protested.

"I know. But it might contain something useful. God knows I don't have many other leads." I tossed some bills on the table. "C'mon. I have to find some aspirins before Eliane's driver comes for me."

We walked down Government Street, past the neat little import shops selling Irish lace, English woolens and china, hand-knitted Cowichan Indian sweaters and the like, and finally found a drugstore. I zipped in to buy drugs while Lester begged a paper cup of water from a pretty blonde waitress in Murchie's Tea Room. We met back on the cobblestones where I swallowed four pills, hoping for relief.

"Say, don't you think you should, you know, go home and rest?" Lester asked, concerned.

"Nah. I'll be okay. You can go on back to your shop for the afternoon. I'll be along later."

"How? Do you want me to come and get you?"

"If no one offers to drive me home, I'll call you," I told him. "Don't fuss."

Out of the shelter of the buildings on Government Street, the wind was chill. I zipped my jacket up to my chin.

"Well, see you later," Lester said tentatively.

I punched him gently in the shoulder. "I'm fine. Go to work."

With a worried smile, he left me.

Thank God. I turned my face into the cold wind, letting it buffet my face, riffle my hair. It felt terrific and I took deep breaths, willing the pain in my head to subside. It did, a little, and I crossed the street, the bulk of the ivy-covered Empress Hotel looming behind me. The expanse of the Inner Harbor now lay before me with the Laurel Point Inn on my far left and the stone breakwater that protected the businesses lining the harbor on my right. Today the water was black, the sky a soft dove-gray, with only a pale line of brightness on the horizon to suggest the presence of sun.

Would spring ever come, I wondered. The rose garden behind the Empress Hotel was already in bud, I'd noticed, and when I closed my eyes I could smell the dark, rich loam of flowerbeds being prepared for planting. I sighed. As I grew older, I found that I craved sunny days, primary colors, representational art, and unambiguous poetry. I had no more patience for subtlety and mysteries.

Feeling remote and disembodied, I leaned against the carved limestone blocks of the seawall and watched a red and white Air BC float plane land at the mouth of the harbor. The wind freshened, whipping the waters of the harbor to whitecaps, and the float plane wallowed like an ungainly bird. I tasted salt spray on my lips and took another deep breath. Good. My headache was definitely fading.

When a car horn sounded behind me, I came back to reality. I turned. A dark green Rolls Royce sedan with vanity plates that said ST CYR was just pulling up to the curb. My ride, presumably. I was impressed. Walking to the car, I found I was a little dizzy. With care, I opened the back door and slid in. The interior was fawn leather, the windows were tinted and, to my enormous surprise, Eliane was sitting against the far door.

"Hello," I said feeling awkward.

"I thought I'd better come and help Sylvie recognize you," she said, smiling. I didn't ask how. There was a window between the front and back seats. It was half open, presumably so the passenger could talk to the chauffeur. Eliane touched a button beside her and the window slid closed. This glass, too, was tinted. Now we were sealed together in the half light of this tiny space and I felt disembodied all over again. The traffic, the cries of seabirds, the whirring of the float plane's props — all these were somewhere far away. I felt as if I had just stepped off the edge of the world. Or through the Looking Glass.

Today Eliane was dressed in a black suede windbreaker, black leather gloves, and black wool pants. I saw the top of a white silk turtleneck above the windbreaker's collar. Her glossy hair was drawn back as severely as ever and today she wore dark glasses. She turned to face me, drawing off the gloves and putting them on the seat beside her, and taking off her glasses. These small gestures seemed terribly intimate and I swallowed, aware all over again of this woman's profound effect on me. Perhaps my mind had refused to provide me with the memory of her for a good reason.

She bent toward me, holding out her hands, and I recognized the scent she had worn the other day. Joy.

I took her hands, noting with surprise that despite the gloves, they were cold. I felt again the long slim fingers, the smooth palms.

"Your hands are warm," Eliane said. "I smell the sea in your hair." She paused. "Thank you for calling."

"I had to," I answered honestly. "I had no choice. There's something going on . . . something that my mind didn't want to deal with. Do you know that it, or I, erased all memory of you for a day and a half?"

She reached up and laid a hand against my cheek, then smoothed my hair, touched my shoulder, and folded her hands together in her lap. Where her fingers had touched my face, I felt that I had been scalded.

"Eliane. What's happening? What's going on? How could Blalock speak to me inside my head?" My voice broke as I asked this question.

"The conventional answer, of course, is that he didn't. What you heard was a memory. He probably stood over you after you were attacked and said those words."

I thought for a minute. "Yeah, maybe. So what's the unconventional answer?"

"I don't think I have to tell you."

"Tell me anyway."

"That, yes, he did speak inside your head."

I looked away from her eyes. "I want to tell you something," I said after a moment. "My mother's family's name is Llewelyn. They're a spooky bunch. Her two older sisters were nutty as almond groves. My Aunt Fiona was certifiable. In the last years of her life she used to sit on a straight-backed kitchen chair at the top of the basement stairs waiting for the Dark Lady. The men in my family thought she was nuts."

"And the women?"

I laughed. "We knew she wasn't. Not exactly. Because what she had, we had, too. All of us. Some more than others. It's a . . . genetic thing. We either accept it and try to make some accommodation with it or we go over the edge."

"What about you? Do you accept it?"

"When I was younger, I denied it. Then, after Aunt Fee died and I started seeing the Dark Lady myself, I thought I was ready for the rubber room. I began to have nightmares in which a figure in black popped out of cupboards and closets and chased me. I knew I was a goner if it ever caught up with me. Well, it didn't, of course. And gradually this obsession faded. I stopped dreaming about dark ladies in the basement and got on with my life."

"Do you ever see the Dark Lady now?"

I looked at Eliane, a tenebrous figure in the gloom, and fought to control my voice. "Not often. But when I do, I recognize her for what she is. A message from . . ." I shrugged. "From where? From no place that makes sense. From chaos. A warning to take care."

Eliane smiled. "What other gifts did the Llewelyns give you?"

"How do you know there are any others?"

"I have a feeling there might be."

I took a deep breath. I'd never talked to anyone else about this. How could I? They'd think I was nuts. "Why don't you think I'm crazy?"

"Because I, too, believe in chaos."

I nodded. "Yes, you do. What other gifts did they give me? Well, a kind of . . . prescience. When I need to, I can sometimes come up with answers I couldn't possibly have acquired logically. I just . . . know things. The knowledge comes all in a flash. It kind of sizzles through my brain." I shrugged. "That's all."

She shook her head. "No. There's more."

The hair lifted on the back of my neck. How could she know?

"When you look into certain pairs of eyes, the eyes of the very worst men you've known, tell me what happens."

I swallowed and my tongue struggled to shape the right words, words I'd never been able to say to anyone. "I feel . . . a jolt. Like a low-voltage charge. My heart seems to shrink. I want to run."

"But you don't."

"No. I don't."

"Why not?"

"Because someone has to say no to them. Because one of those someones is me."

She was silent for a moment. "Have you ever thought that you didn't choose to be one of those someones?"

"Didn't choose? What do you mean?"

"What I mean is, perhaps saying no chose you."

"I . . . what are you saying? That we don't have free will? That there's some secret screenplay already typed double-spaced sitting on some celestial director's desk, and I'm just playing my part?"

"Why does the prospect offend you so much?"

I shook my head again, unable to shape my thoughts into words.

"Listen to me," she said, bending toward me. "I'm very fond of the notion of balances. If we admit that there's such a thing as evil in the world — capital E evil — and I think that's something we both believe, then we have to admit that there's such a thing as good. Capital G good."

I said nothing.

"Well?"

Reluctantly, I said, "I'd like to think so. God knows I'd like to think that's so. Good, beauty, love, the things that count . . . yes, I'd like to think they really do exist. As much as evil, ugliness, and hatred."

"Of course they do," she whispered. "How can you doubt?" Then, "Don't you know what you are?"

"What?"

"If I were religious, I'd say you were one of God's warriors. An angel with a sword. Michael. But alas, I gave up on religion a long time ago. So I'll just call you a force for good. With your prescience and your water-witch instinct for evil and your craving for the bright and the beautiful, how could you be anything else?"

I looked at this woman. Who was she? What made her think she knew anything about me? I shook my head. "I don't think so," I told her. "I'm just . . . someone who wants to help."

She nodded. "Of course you do. Of course you do."

And that seemed to be that. We drove the rest of the way to her house in silence. And as we drove, I tried to bring my wandering wits to bear on what was surely the most extraordinary situation I had ever been in. Although I had called Eliane a Froot Loop to Repo, there was a part of me — a very large part of me — that resonated to her, that knew that what she talked about — monsters, evil, good, angels with swords — was all true. And that part of me knew, too, that if I let her she would point me at Fell/Blalock like a fiery arrow, like a silver bullet, like Jove's thunderbolt. But did I want to let her? Did I want to make her fight my own? I groaned. I just wanted enough information to find Laura. And Blalock. Or Fell. Or whatever he was calling himself now. And to close this case. God. Why did it have to be so . . . complicated?

I turned my head to look at Eliane and suddenly it was all very simple. What she wanted from me — what I sensed she wanted from me — was so inextricably tied to my desire for her that I knew if I said yes to one thing, I would be unable to deny her anything at all. Maybe what the animal behaviorists say is true — that sexual attraction is largely based on pheromones. That desire is olfactory. And that, most interestingly, we lust after those who smell like our litter mates. Like ourselves.

Was she like me? I doubted it. But whatever the answer, I knew that Eliane's attraction for me was barely deniable. I had to get my information and run. Otherwise . . . otherwise what? What was I afraid of? I closed my eyes and turned my head away.

"Do you feel ill?" Eliane asked.

"My head," I answered, glad to be able to talk about a physical, rather than a psychic, ache.

"I will have Agathe make you a *tisane,*" she said. "Then you will feel better."

I wasn't sure about that, but for form's sake, I assented. "Okay," I said.

Locked in our thoughts, we drove the rest of the way in silence.

Surprisingly, Agathe's *tisane* worked. I felt pretty darned good. Good enough, I hoped, to find what I needed and go before I'd have to deal with the howlings of my libido.

Romany — a bizarre twenty-five-year-old lass with spiked crimson hair, a baggy black T-shirt, black tights, and black lace-up boots — brought an armful of files into the library and stacked them on the coffee table, moving things around to make room. Evidently very fond of Eliane, she fussed over her, making sure she knew the new location of rearranged items.

"The stereo remote is on the lamp table," she told her, guiding her hand. "Your notebook computer is beside it, there," she said.

"I've found them," Eliane said, smiling at her, kissing her cheek. "Caitlin and I are going to spend the afternoon together working. Perhaps the evening, too. You may take one of the cars into town if you like."

"Nah," Romany told her, blowing enthusiastic bubble-gum bubbles. "I'll transcribe what you recorded last night. I might take the weekend off. Go over to Galiano and see a friend." She gave me a frank stare. "Just call downstairs if you need anything."

"What do you think of Romany?" Eliane asked me when the girl had gone.

"Interesting," I equivocated.

"She's Agathe's daughter. She always was a strange child — reclusive, brilliant. But extremely withdrawn and anti-social. We despaired of her future. But fortunately for us, she became enamored of computers. She communicates with people all over the world now by means of electronic bulletin boards. She transcribes my notes, tinkers with her equipment. She seems happy. And she's a great help to me."

"She's very fond of you," I said.

"And I of her," Eliane said. "But come, sit. You have a lot of material to read."

I sat down on the couch and Eliane came to sit in her place on the sofa perpendicular to it. "I'll get you started," she said, "and then I'll just let you read. I'll listen to music, if you don't mind."

"I don't mind."

"What would you like to hear? What wouldn't distract you?"

I almost laughed out loud. *What wouldn't distract me is if you left the room. Or maybe the planet,* I thought. Instead, I gave a reasonable answer. "I have great powers of concentration. You choose." *Besides, I'm not going to be here long. I don't dare.*

"Perhaps I'll just pick up where I left off this morning with some Chopin. It might be better if I used the headphones. Oh, the file folder that has most of the important information in it — details about Fell's childhood and so on — should be on top. We have a copy machine downstairs in Romany's computer room. You can copy anything you want. There's a fax, too, I understand. The number is the same as mine, plus one."

I picked up one of the sharpened pencils Romany had left and pulled a yellow lined tablet onto my lap. "Pencil and paper will probably be enough. Oh, and I'd like a phone, too."

"There's a portable phone on the desk in the corner. Anything else?"

"No. Thanks."

"Let me know if you need me." Donning the stereo headphones, she punched some buttons on the remote, put her head back comfortably on the couch, and presumably tuned back into Chopin.

I picked up the file folder and started reading. At various points, Agathe came into the library and made a fire, Romany came and went on suspiciously transparent errands, and a beautiful sable Burmese cat visited briefly to twine around my ankles. But I was only half-aware of these visitations. When I have to, I can totally immerse myself in my reading. And I can read very fast, too. Anyone who lasted more than the three-month trial period with the CP had to be able to read like a demon and retain everything. I cursed the fact that the sketchy information I possessed on Theo Blalock was at home — his arrest record and the information Laura had given me. Nevertheless, I thought I could recall it.

When my eyes were too tired to read anymore, I put the folder down. Could Theo Blalock be Martin Fell? What commonalities did they share? Theo Blalock was, supposedly, twenty-three. Martin Fell was twenty-five. Big deal. When Fell changed names he could have changed his age too, just to muddy the waters. Both men had had scrapes with the law. I shook my head. That wasn't much to go on.

Eight years ago, when Fell had attacked Eliane, he had been seventeen, a juvie, in custody for burglary. I wondered what in hell had possessed him to attack her, thereby earning himself twelve years in the youth authority for attempted murder. That was beside the point, however. If he'd been sentenced to twelve years in the YA, he'd still be there. Therefore, no way could he be Theo Blalock. That seemed to be something easily verified. I looked at my watch. Just before four. The authorities at the YA on the mainland ought to be still semi-conscious.

I looked over at Eliane's couch. Gone.

"This is the Crown Prosecutor's office," I said to a bored-sounding male who answered the phone at the YA. "Assistant CP Caitlin Reece here. I'd like to speak to someone in Records."

"Just a minute," he said, and soon an equally bored-sounding female voice came on the line.

"Miss Renquist. Records."

"Hi, Miss Renquist. This is Caitlin Reece at the CP's office on the island. I know this is a little irregular, but could you pull a record for us?"

"Wellll," she said, clearly uncomfortable. "I don't know. What do you need?"

"We just need to establish something," I told her. "One of our, ah, defendants has given this name as his alibi but we have information that he's serving time with you."

"Oh, well, *that* should be easy to find out," she said, clearly relieved that nothing terribly irregular was going to be asked of her. "What's the name?"

"Fell. Martin Fell."

"We're computerized now," she said. "I'll just punch it in." Silence. Then: "Well, it looks like your alibi might be true. Fell was released, oh, ten months ago."

"Thanks," I said automatically and hung up.

Shit. Ten months. Hadn't Renata Sethi said that Blalock had lived on Arbutus for about a year? And Sandy told me that the cops had been called out to Blalock's twice during their marriage. And Laura had only been married to him for a year.

I sat back. Oh, hell. Maybe it all fit. Maybe Blalock was Fell, after all. I closed my eyes. Why hadn't the Ferret gotten back to me with information on Blalock? Was it because there really wasn't any? I picked up the portable phone and dialed The Ferret's number. As I expected, I got his recording.

"Do I know you? If I do, leave a message and I'll call you back. If I don't, don't."

"Ferret, it's Caitlin. I need the dope on Blalock. And I need it now. Whatever you've got. You've had days and days to twiddle your sources. I'm at this fax number. I'm waiting."

I hung up and gnawed a hangnail. If Blalock was really Fell, this junior monster grown up, then the photo thing certainly fit. I guessed he and Laura could have been planning extortion. But why had the photos frightened Laura so much? I closed my eyes. It was as if she hadn't known a thing about them. But that was crazy. She plainly knew enough to be terrified. But of whom? I threw my pencil down on the couch in disgust.

And if she wasn't working with Theo, running a nice little extortion scam, then who the hell had clobbered me the other morning? I'd assumed it was Laura. And where was she if she hadn't run back to Blalock/Fell as soon as I entered the case?

Think, I told myself. Just think. What do you know? That Laura about lost it when she saw the photos. That Laura and Theo had had several acrimonious exchanges in the past couple of weeks. That Laura had run away. That Theo was missing, too. I massaged my eyes. It didn't add up. Even assuming Blalock *was* Fell.

What did I know about Fell, anyhow?

Martin Fell, born Christmas Day, twenty-five years ago in Prince Rupert, British Columbia. A nice little piece of irony, that. Father Patrick Fell, mother Maude Devlin. Irish immigrant families, both. Fell Sr. worked in the logging industry. The mother, Maude, had been a schoolteacher. Until she became a drunk. Fell started his life of crime early, it seemed — beating up his fellow classmates, stealing their lunch money or items of their clothing he fancied, stealing a bicycle from the local sporting goods shop, stealing a camera, and finally embarking on a spree of vandalizing school property which included killing the animals in the science lab. He was also fond of setting fires. Remarks in his school file noted that discipline from home was "erratic to nonexistent."

I flipped pages. Fell's IQ was very high — 141 on the last test he had taken. As high as his grades were low. When he struck a teacher who was attempting to discipline him, he was expelled. Fell Sr. was injured in a logging accident and the family moved to Vancouver when Martin was sixteen. With his insurance money, Fell Sr. sent Martin to live with a relative in Victoria where Martin was enrolled in private school. That lasted less than a year. Martin was much fonder of burglarizing his classmates' parents' homes than he was of attending school, it seemed. He ended up in juvie hall when he was so careless as to have shown one classmate some of the things he'd taken from another classmate's home — some photos, apparently. That was when Eliane entered the picture.

I set the file down. Why would Fell have struck her? According to Eliane's notes, she had interviewed him on three previous occasions without incident. What exactly had happened during that last interview? I made a note to ask her. I also made notes about the name of Martin's teacher at the private school, the Oak Bay police sergeant who had taken Fell into custody, and a teacher at Fell's school in Prince Rupert, Emily Weaver, who insisted on appending a statement to his file. The statement, curiously enough, was nowhere to be found. Well, the file was eight years old. Anything could have happened to a single piece of paper.

But there was absolutely nothing in this first folder that suggested where Fell might be now. The information was eight years out of date. The trail was cold. Did the family still live in Prince Rupert? I made a note to inquire. And the relative in Victoria? I made a note to inquire about that, too.

The chances of locating Fell were, I realized, less than fifty-fifty. Ex-cons usually hot-foot it back to the neighborhoods they lived in before they were arrested. But Fell? Would he have gone back to live with the Victoria relative? I doubted it. Where then? Home? That seemed unlikely. After all, Fell Sr. had sent him away. No, it was more likely that he was now hanging out with one of the fine upstanding examples of Canadian youth that he had met in prison, continuing the life of theft, burglary, and violence that Eliane had interrupted. But continuing it as Theo Blalock?

What I needed was information on Blalock. I needed his juvenile file, if he had one. I needed his school records. I needed to develop a file on him and see if the holes could be filled in by facts from Martin Fell's background, like one of those transparent anatomy overlays in a medical textbook.

Why in hell didn't the Ferret call? I was certainly paying him enough money. I put the file folder down and rubbed my eyes. My headache was back. Looking around, I realized that Eliane had not returned. I was quite alone in the library. And the afternoon had turned to dusk. What was the poetic term for it? Darkling. A good adjective, that. Outside the window, it seemed that whatever feeble sunshine the day had granted us was now concentrated in a startling bright band on the horizon. A ribbon of gold strung between a dark gray ocean and a darker sky. And thinking of dusk made me think of the lines from Matthew Arnold's "Dover Beach," the part where he asserts that the world

> Hath really neither joy nor love nor light
> Nor certitude, nor peace, nor help for pain;
> And we are here as on a darkling plain
> Swept with confused alarms of struggle
>   and flight,
> Where ignorant armies clash by night.

Was he right? Who knew. Sometimes I certainly thought so. I touched my fingers to the glass as if to gather in the bright ribbon of gold. But it faded to lemon yellow as I watched, then to dun, and so to dark.

Hearing a noise behind me, I turned. It was Eliane.

"Caitlin?"

"Over here," I told her. "By the window."

She came to lean against the back of the sofa. About six feet separated us. She crossed her arms over her breasts. I noticed that she had thrown a black shawl over her shoulders and fastened it with a silver pin. "Did you finish reading the files?" she asked.

"The one on Fell. And the one with your transcript notes. I haven't read the file on your predictive design."

"Do you think you can find him? Fell?"

"I don't know," I told her honestly. "The trail's old. There are a lot of questions to ask. But the file has given me a number of good leads. I'll have to get to work on them."

"Is he . . . this Blalock person? The one you're looking for?"

"I can't tell that yet. I have someone researching the facts I need on Theo Blalock. Francis, my . . . associate, has been working to assemble a file. I've asked him to fax me some information here."

"And then you'll know?"

"And then I might know, yes."

She seemed to think about this for a moment, then roused herself and walked toward me. "Was there a sunset?"

I was surprised at the change of subject. "No. Just some brightness on the horizon."

She held out her hand as she approached and I took it. I was not particularly surprised when she did not let mine go.

"Will you stay for supper?" she asked. "Agathe will serve it soon. I usually take it in here."

I turned to face her. She was so close that our clasped hands brushed my thigh. I would only have to incline my head, to bend just a little, to kiss her.

"If you want to stay, I'd like that very much," she said.

No, I can't, I wanted to say. *I'm not your angel with the sword, your avenging spirit. I'm just me, a tired, wounded, and not particularly smart investigator. And I'm involved with someone else. Someone good and kind who probably loves me. I don't want to get mixed up with this obsession of yours. I just want the answer to a very simple question, not the cosmic unraveling that you seem to seek.* Instead, to my amazement, I heard myself answer, "Yes. I'll stay."

At Eliane's request, I stirred the fire and placed a couple of pine logs on the andirons. Agathe brought us a bottle of wine and two glasses, placing them on the coffee table, and Eliane poured the Merlot for us. Perhaps I was in one of my head-injured fugue states, but all this seemed to be happening in a dream. I sat on my couch, drinking wine, completely incapable of conversation, and Eliane sat on hers. The fire crackled and spat and, behind me, I heard Agathe setting one of the small mahogany tables for dinner.

"How do you feel?" Eliane asked.

I swallowed the giggle that threatened to burst in my throat. "Odd," I said, putting my wineglass down. "I don't think I ought to be drinking."

"You need food. You need to eat," Eliane said. "Come, let's start dinner."

What I needed more than dinner, I realized, was to go home to bed. I felt . . . shaky. Feeble. Mortal. I needed to take care of myself. I needed to curl up with a couple of cats. But dammit, how was I going to say this to Eliane? She clearly had other plans for me. We sat at the little table Agathe had prepared. A clear soup was waiting for us in white bowls with gold rims. I unfolded my heavy linen napkin, spread it on my lap, and picked up my soup spoon, wondering desperately how I would make it through this meal. Fortunately, the problem was solved for me.

"Eliane, I'm sorry," Romany apologized, materializing at her elbow. "A phone call. For Caitlin. You can take it on the portable," she told me.

As I got up to walk to Eliane's desk, I raised an eyebrow. Who on earth could be calling me here?

"Caitlin? It's Lester," a worried-sounding voice said. "Listen, I'm here at your place and I just heard a phone message that Liz left for you. She says Laura called. She's real upset. Wants to talk. She's at a restaurant — you know, that pancake place at Cedar Hill Cross? She wants Liz to meet her there."

"Call Liz," I told Lester. "Tell her definitely not to go. Meet me there but stay outside. I'm on my way."

"Trouble?" Eliane asked as I hung up.

"Yeah. Things are breaking loose. At last." I paced a little, thinking.

"You need to go," Eliane said. The statement was not a question.

"Yes. I do. And I need to borrow a car."

"Sylvie —"

"No. I don't know what's going to happen. I don't want the responsibility of Sylvie's being there."

Eliane nodded. "There are three cars in the garage. Romany will show you the way. Take whichever one you want."

"Thanks," I said. "I'm sorry I have to run off. But this is important. I think Liz, my client, is being lured into a trap."

"By Fell?"

"Maybe. Or by Blalock. He's using Laura to reel Liz in." But why? Why?

"Go, then," Eliane said.

But I dithered. Something more seemed to be required of me. "I —"

"Just go," Eliane repeated. Then she smiled, just a little. "I, too, sense things are 'breaking loose,' as you put it. If you want to, and if you are able, you will come back. Go now."

Unwilling to puzzle out the ambiguities of her remark, I went.

The parking lot of the pancake house at Cedar Hill Cross was almost empty. I spotted Lester's Samurai right away, parked three slots down from a little white car which I recognized as Laura's Camry. I pulled my borrowed black Mercedes in next to Lester, got out, and motioned for him to roll down his window.

"Stay here," I told him, cutting off his questions. "Keep your eyes open and your doors locked. If Liz shows up, don't let her go in there. I'll be back."

The interior of the pancake house was bright and warm. Orange vinyl seats, blonde wood, plants. Cheery. Precisely the opposite of my mood. Laura was sitting at a booth in the far corner of the restaurant and when she saw me come through the door, she half rose, as if to bolt. I shook my head and she subsided.

"You look like shit," I told her as I ordered coffee and a large plate of fries. And she did. Her hair was lank and greasy, her clothes were rumpled, as though they'd been slept in, and she looked as though she'd jump out of her skin at the first loud noise. "What's up?"

"I expected Liz," she said diffidently.

"I told her not to come. You can tell me what you would have told her." The waitress brought coffee and I added cream and sugar. The fries followed and I shoveled them in, thinking ruefully of my interrupted romantic dinner. "Talk, Laura. I'm a whisker away from Blalock," I invented. "And when I find him, I'm going to see that he's charged with assault, attempted extortion, and anything else I can think of."

"Assault? On whom?"

I looked closely. Damn. She really didn't know. "On me."

Her eyes darted away. This woman's scared to death, I realized.

"Tell me all of it," I said. "From the beginning."

"Okay." She nodded, as if coming to a decision. "Okay." Twisting her napkin into a pretzel shape, she looked up at me once, quickly, then down at the table. "It was going to be extortion. You were right. Theo and I . . . it was his idea. We needed money. He needed money. For that stupid boat of his." She closed her eyes. "With him, it's always some damned big scheme or other. Some scheme that never works. I should never have married him."

"A boat?"

"A trawler. His father left it to him last year when he died. It's in drydock. It needs about fifty thousand in repairs to make it seaworthy." She took a deep breath. "I had just met Liz. She had the landscape contract at my school. Things weren't going so well between Theo and me. I used to talk to her. She was . . . sympathetic. I ran away from Theo and went to stay with Liz. I don't know what happened but I ended up in bed with her one night."

What a crock. Of course she knew.

"What happened with Liz, well, I was frightened. I . . . went back to Theo. You don't know him, but he can be really charming. Really nice." She looked up at me, begging for understanding. I didn't give it to her. She ducked her head and continued. "I told him what happened and that's when he got this idea. That I would go and live with Liz, that I would make her . . . you know, fond of me, protective . . ." She trailed off. "Do you know how hard this is?" she asked. "You're not making it any easier sitting there like a damned statue!"

"Sorry," I lied. "I'm sure it is hard. Please go on. So you went to live with Liz. When was this?"

"About four months ago. Just before Christmas. We were going to start hitting Liz up for money in April."

I sat up straight. "What happened? Liz said the first photo came in the middle of March."

She looked up at me with haunted eyes. "That's just it. We hadn't planned on doing anything like that. When I found the photos in Liz's truck, I was . . ." She broke off and put her hands over her face. Combing her hair with her fingers, she straightened up, sniffled, and continued. "When I found the photos, I was horrified. Theo and I had two terrible fights about them. You see, Theo was just going to, well, blackmail Liz. Tell her he'd leave her alone, leave us alone, if she'd pay up."

"I don't get it. Why did he send photos instead?"

"He didn't," she whispered. "Theo didn't send the photos."

A terrible premonition laid an icy hand on the back of my neck. "Who, Laura? Who's sending them, then?"

"Martin Fell," she stammered, her teeth chattering in terror. "Theo's cousin, Martin Fell."

Chapter 10

The hot tea I'd ordered for Laura had stopped her teeth from chattering but her hands shook so badly I had to pour a refill. "It's not Liz he wants," she gibbered. "The photos have nothing to do with Liz. It's me — he wants me!"

"Shh," I said, wondering what in hell to do to stem Laura's rising hysteria. I needed her coherent. "How can you be sure?"

She laughed. "Listen. All three of us were in private school together. Martin was living with Theo's family. He was sixteen, Theo and I were both fourteen. And he was . . . horrible. I can't tell you how horrible. It's like he had no heart. No soul. But he was smart, so smart. And charming." She swallowed. "Anyhow, he . . . stole things. From houses."

"Burglaries? Breaking and entering?"

She nodded. "Yes. That was part of the fun, he said. And he made Theo help him. But Martin never really took anything . . . sensible."

I felt cold. "What do you mean, sensible."

She blushed. "He never took stereos or TVs or anything he could sell. Or use. He took, well, underwear, pantyhose, things like that."

"And photos," I added.

She looked at me in surprise. "Yes. And photos. That's how he got caught, you know. He was making one of those photo things he used to assemble and one of our friends, David Summers, recognized the people in the photos. David told the boy whose house had been burglarized, he told his parents, and the police came for Martin the next day." She shivered. "He never came home again. God. I was so glad. And we — Theo and I — gradually forgot about him. I just wanted to put all that behind me. In fact, once we graduated, I didn't even see Theo again until I ran into him in a pub, oh, about a year ago. He'd just been left the trawler in his father's will and he was so excited about it."

I was too impatient to hear about Theo and Laura's budding romance. There was an answer, a truth, just beyond my grasp and dammit, I wanted it. "So when did Theo hear from Fell. March?"

"No. Earlier. Much earlier. And Theo kept it from me. He knew he'd better!" she said vehemently.

"Why?"

"Because I hated Martin. He tried . . . he tried to rape me. When I was fourteen. He was jealous of me. At least I always thought so. Theo was his little slave, following him around, doing whatever he wanted. Theo worshipped Martin. But I didn't. And he knew that." She laughed but there was no speck of mirth in the laughter. "One night we were all at Theo's house. His parents were out. I was talking to Theo in the kitchen, trying to tell him to cool it with Martin. Martin overheard me and was furious. Anyway, he sent Theo to the store for something — can you believe it? And when Theo was gone he tried to rape me. But he couldn't! He couldn't get an erection." She poured more tea, her hands a little steadier. "I'll never forget his rage, his insane rage, and the look on his face. He said he'd kill me if I told anyone and I believe he would have." She shook her head. "I stopped hanging around with Theo after that. A couple of weeks later, Martin was arrested. I couldn't have been happier."

"Until you found out about the photos."

"Yes," she said in a very small voice. "Until then." She closed her eyes and tears rolled down her cheeks. "I'm not proud of what Theo and I planned to do to Liz. To blackmail her."

No kidding. I all but bit my tongue to keep from saying something I'd regret.

"But this photo thing!" She lowered her voice. "Martin used to send those photo collages to people whose houses he'd broken into to . . . scare them. He hated them. He'd study the houses, study the people, the women, for weeks. The mothers and sisters of his classmates. Then he'd break in and steal things. And he always took photos."

"Photos that he'd turn around and send back. Assembled a little differently," I added.

"Yes."

"Laura?"

She looked up from her napkin twisting.

"Why do you think Martin is sending you these pictures?"

She squeezed her eyes shut. "Because he's sending me a message. Just like the mothers and sisters of his classmates. He hated them and he hates me. Except he has a much better reason to hate me than he did to hate them. He's telling me to keep away from Theo. To leave them alone. He used Theo in the old days and he wants to use him again. I guess," she concluded on a far from certain note. For my part, I said nothing. Telling her what Eliane believed Martin to be would only send her over the edge. I decided to change the subject slightly.

"Okay." I signaled the waitress for more coffee. Eating had helped my headache. Now I needed caffeine. "Talk to me about Theo. About his part in the extortion."

She made an impatient gesture. "Theo's weak. Handsome and charming, but weak. When I saw him after all those years, well, I fell for him all over again. I would have done whatever he wanted. The trawler, the money, Liz . . . I'll never forgive myself for saying yes. Because Liz is a good person, a really good person. Even before I knew Martin was back, I went to the cannery two weeks ago and told Theo that I couldn't go through with it. You know what?" She laughed. "He called me a dyke. A lesbian. Said Liz had corrupted me. Well, I'll tell you something. I had more kindness from Liz in the months I lived with her than the year I lived with Theo. I told him that, too. She's a fine, generous person. An achiever. A success. She works hard. God, what we'd planned was crazy. Terrible." She wiped her eyes with the back of her hand. "But I think, no, I *know,* that Martin has Theo under his spell again." She looked at me, her eyes hopeless. "He's gone. He moved his stuff out of his apartment. They're holed up together. Somewhere. And Martin's turned Theo against me, just like he tried to do when we were kids. But this time, he's done it."

I sat back, drinking coffee. It made sense. It finally all made sense. I wasn't happy with the sense it made — I'd much rather not have to chase a creep like Fell — but my desire for logic had been served.

"Do you think Liz is in danger?" Laura asked in a small voice, interrupting my thoughts.

I shook my head. "I don't think so. It's you Fell wants. And now that we know all about it, the extortion thing is off."

Clearly relieved, Laura nodded, examining the depths of her teacup. I studied her, wondering how Theo could just sit back and let Fell do this horrible thing to the woman he supposedly loved. Or was he so pissed off with Laura that he didn't care? After all, she was the one who derailed the extortion scheme. I wondered, too, if he really knew what Martin had planned for Laura — the ending of the script that Eliane asserted he'd been writing since childhood. I felt frustrated that I'd never had a chance to talk to him, or gotten a feel for how his mind worked. It might have been possible to play Theo off against Fell, to drive a wedge between them.

"Where are you staying?" I asked Laura.

"Staying? Nowhere. Theo knows all of my friends, where my parents live. I'm sure Martin has wormed all that out of him. I just . . . drive around."

"I know someplace you'll be safe," I told her. "You need to stop running. And trust me, Theo couldn't find out about this place in a year of trying. Finish your tea and we'll go."

"What are you going to do now?" Laura wanted to know.

I felt the back of my head. "Find the bastards. Both of them."

"And then?"

"Then we'll see. I'm sure that Fell has done something to violate his parole. And if he hasn't, I'll see that he does. You leave Fell to me."

Brave words, Caitlin. Brave words.

Chapter 11

While Jory took an exhausted Laura to Gray's guest room, I apologized again for the lateness of the hour and the inconvenience.

"I know your place isn't the hospice of the Pacific Northwest," I said. "But I'm fresh out of ideas. This lady needs a safe place to stay for a day or two. Put her to work. I'm sure she can do something."

Gray held up a hand. "We'll manage. I'll help Jory."

A pair of table lamps made pools of golden light

beside two easy chairs in Gray's living room. I occupied one and Lester the other. I dearly wanted to close my eyes and never open them again. Instead, my mind raced, planning tomorrow's activities. One of The Girls, Gray's enormous brindled Great Danes, took up a post by the door; the other came to lay an enormous head on my knees. Lester cleared his throat.

"Now what?" he wanted to know, eyeing The Girls warily.

"Now we go home to bed." I checked my watch. Well after midnight. "It's far too late to do anything tonight."

"And tomorrow?"

"Tomorrow we find Blalock and Fell. According to Laura, they're holed up somewhere together. Fell's just out of prison and Blalock doesn't have any money so it's my guess that they're with friends. Maybe one of those boxes we carted away from Arbutus Street will talk to us. Or maybe The Ferret will have come up with something. I'll call a few of the names I wrote down after reading Fell's file. They might be able to suggest something useful." I fixed Lester with a stern look. "It's good old-fashioned boring detective work tomorrow, junior. Reading. Sorting. Thinking."

Squaring his shoulders, he nodded. Clearly, he was ready for anything. Even boredom. He might make an investigator yet.

"Gray's finally got that garage of hers finished," I told him. "Do you want to put Eliane's Mercedes in it? I'll ride home with you — your last chance to play chauffeur. Tomorrow, I drive." I tossed him Eliane's keys. Giving The Girl at the door a wide berth, he sidled out. I smiled. Cautious Lester. On second thought, maybe he wouldn't make an investigator.

"Jory is going to prepare sandwiches for Miss Neal," Gray said from the kitchen. "She could certainly benefit from some food." She came to lean against the doorjamb. "What about you?"

"Um, no thanks," I told her. "I'm too distracted to sit down and be polite. Lester and I will grab something on the highway."

"How are you feeling?"

I shrugged. "All right. Tired. My head aches. I'll be glad to get home."

"Perhaps you ought to have spent today gathering your strength."

I bristled, stemming the tide of angry words that rushed to my lips. I had a job to do, dammit, but it seemed that everyone, well-meaning or not, wanted to keep me from it. What was I supposed to do — take to my bed like a Victorian matron with the vapors?

As if she sensed my irritation, Gray said with a smile, "To be an angel with a sword is a terrible burden. You will need all your strength for it."

For an instant I felt the world slipping again. Had I told Gray what Eliane had said? I must have — otherwise how could she know? I decided not to ask.

She looked at me unblinkingly. "Being injured often serves to remind us of our mortality. The farther away from life we wander the more precious it becomes when we are born into it again." She cocked her head on one side. "When you lay in the hospital for a day, unconscious, what do you recall from that time?"

"Nothing. It's just a big piece subtracted from my life. It was . . . unconsciousness." She continued to look at me. "Wasn't it?"

"I don't think so."

"Oh?"

"Life becomes very simple. Loyalty, work, love — the things that are important call a little more loudly to us." When I said nothing, she continued. "If we are wise, we listen to the call. For those of us who have . . . come back, our lives are twice-given gifts. They are very precious. We must be careful about who we loan them to." She paused. "Who have you loaned yours to?"

I swallowed. "A . . . woman." Then, in as few words as possible, I told her about Eliane and Martin Fell. When I was done, she stood silent, unmoving, eyes focused on nothing. Then she seemed to shake herself, to come back from some distant place. "You are in the hands of a woman whose heart, whose soul, belongs to the struggle with our ancient enemy, the dragon. With monsters in human form. With the goblin men. This is what she loves. Do you think that you can go to the goblin market and buy her soul back? You cannot, not even with the coin of your courage. Liz thinks this, too — that she can face down the goblins, barter for Laura's soul but she, also, is mistaken. We give our souls away, or keep them, as we will. Eliane's particular struggle with the dragon is not yours. Do not assume the role of her champion. You have your own battles ahead and must stand aside from hers."

"It's too late to stand aside," I told her, trying unsuccessfully not to be irritated at all this metaphysical mother-henning. "Eliane wants Martin Fell for a different reason than I do." Gray raised her eyebrows, irritating me further. "Dammit, I'm not doing this for her!" But my words sounded hollow, even to me. Half-truths usually do.

"You are chasing the shadow," Gray said. "Do you really think you will catch it?"

I thought of Martin Fell's cruel face, his avid eyes, and shivered. "I don't know. I hope so. But I don't know. I may catch Fell, but sometimes I think . . . about all the other Fells."

"They will always be there," Gray said. "Long after you and I are gone, they will be there."

I put my head back and closed my eyes. "Then it's all futile, isn't it?"

"Is it?"

"I don't know, Gray. I don't think I know anymore. When I started this business, it all seemed pretty simple. But now . . ." I trailed off.

"Now people expect things of you. They have created you with their expectations, named you with their needs. You are their warrior."

"Oh yeah? What if I don't want to be?"

"Ah yes. What, then?"

Feeling irritated all over again, I opened my eyes. "As long as we're being mystical, what are you? A witch? The village wise woman?"

Gray laughed. "Perhaps. I was fired from my last job for being a 'damned Asian witch.' "

"Yeah, I remember."

"You give me too much credit, Caitlin," Gray said. "The truth is, we are both on a journey. It is my curse that I can see your road more clearly than I can see my own."

I looked at her, wondering for the hundredth time who this woman really was. "And what do you see?"

She smiled but said nothing, as I had known she would. I decided to try another tack.

"Why can you see it so clearly?"

"Because it was my road, once, not so long ago. The warrior's road. A very seductive one for those who choose it."

"Seductive?"

"Yes. Because along that road, we are sure to meet the dragon. And encounters with the dragon are always seductive."

"I still don't understand what you mean."

She looked at me for a moment and I thought she was going to answer me with silence — a typical Gray response. But she surprised me. "Don't you see — it is the struggle itself that is seductive. The fight. And the warrior cannot turn aside from it. She cannot see the other road. The other way."

"The other road?" I snorted. "You're not talking about turning the other cheek, are you? Letting the bad guys walk away? Giving them another chance? *Understanding* them?"

She smiled. "No. I am not talking about that."

I looked at her in exasperation, wanting to ask any one of a dozen questions that formed in my mind, but I felt that they wouldn't be answered to my satisfaction. With Gray, one answer just led to another question. And I had no time tonight for more metaphysics. As much as she might disapprove, I was halfway down the road that led to my dragon.

Standing aside, looking for another way, was not an option.

"All squared away!" Lester said, coming into the front hall and closing the door behind him. "Oops," he said, stopping dead in his tracks when The Girls loped to meet him.

Gray whistled softly and the dogs raised their heads, left Lester, and went at once to her side.

"I'm ready," I told Lester. "Thanks," I called to Gray over my shoulder.

Her lips might have twitched in a smile. I couldn't tell. It didn't matter.

FRIDAY

Chapter 12

The sounds of happy avian peeping outside my bedroom window woke me — my apple tree's resident robins setting up their annual spring housekeeping. I cracked open an eyelid and saw a flood of butterscotch sunshine on the oak floor, two cats asleep in it. Surely the subject of a haiku if ever I saw one. But that was Gray's province, not mine. Tossing off the covers, I dragged my weary body out of bed and straightened up carefully. Not too bad. No real dizziness. Just that maddeningly persistent sense of being disembodied, of being not quite here. I smiled. Would Gray assert that a part of me was indeed not here, but back there in the shadow-world?

Sometimes after a particularly vivid dream, I could persuade myself that the world of dreams was the reality and our so-called reality the stuff of dreams. Who knew, anyhow? Certainly the activities of our day-to-day lives were no more bizarre than the stuff of dreams. Maybe there really *was* a world in which we rode naked on the subway, coupled indiscriminately with our co-workers, murdered our siblings, conversed with animals, and flew out our windows on the nights the moon was dark. Then, when we wearied of these activities we could sleep and, sleeping, dream ourselves into a mechanistic world of cause and effect, where logic was lord and nature had laws, where we rode the subway dressed for our jobs, harbored well-banked lust for our co-workers and hatred for our siblings, only patted our pets, and closed the windows on nights when the moon was dark. Again, who knew?

I padded out to the kitchen to start coffee and, as I passed Lester's open bedroom door, glanced inside. He was up, showered and shaved, pressed and dressed, with the contents of Blalock's cartons piled into tiny cairns around the room.

"Hi," he said somewhat self-consciously.

"Hi, yourself. Found any clues?"

"Not yet. But he left behind quite an interesting collection of stuff."

"Oh yeah?"

"Yeah. Bank statements, cancelled checks, tax records, credit card statements, car repair records, phone bills — that sort of thing. There ought to be *something* in here, don't you think?"

"If we're lucky." I yawned. "Had breakfast?"

He nodded. "Fed the cats, too."

I smiled and continued on to the kitchen to start coffee. Pansy chirped at me from the pantry and I opened the door to let her out into Malcolm and Yvonne's garden-to-be. Grabbing a container of yogurt from the kitchen, I took a quick peek at my telephone recorder. Nada. What game was The Ferret playing, anyhow? And Tonia hadn't called, either. Well, presumably she was still as pissed off with me as I had been with her. Aggravated, I went through the house pulling up blinds and opening a few windows. Yup. Spring was definitely on the way. Sunshine and flowers. The siren song of hope. I ate my yogurt staring out the front window at my neighbor weeding his riotously colorful bed of daffodils, freesias, tulips, and hyacinths. I thought of the beginning of T.S. Eliot's poem, "The Waste Land," where he asserts that April is the cruellest month, coaxing lilacs out of the dead earth, mingling desire with memory, bringing sleeping roots to life with spring rain.

Then, feeling like a spoilsport, a traitor to all my neighbor's horticultural hard work which, admittedly, gave me great aesthetic enjoyment, I shunted these thoughts aside. The sun was shining, the flowers were abloom. Surely that was enough. Besides, there was work to be done. No time for angst.

I left Lester sorting and, folding myself into the familiar confines of my MG, roared off in pursuit of Martin Fell. There was one Blalock listed in the phone book — an Elizabeth Blalock — and in the hopes that she was Martin's aunt and would indeed talk to me, I set off. God knew, I didn't have any other leads.

But first, I had to stop at Liz's. She deserved to know what was happening.

4 U I MOW was just being loaded with flats of peach and violet pansies by a denim-clad lass with braids who looked about sixteen. She eyed me frankly as I parked my MG and walked up to Liz's front door. Liz answered my ring at once, saw who it was, and fairly hauled me inside.

"Goddamn you, Reece! I thought you'd just disappeared. We can talk right here in the hall. I don't want the kid to hear my business. So? Why haven't you gotten back to me? I'm paying you, for Christ's sake!" She crossed her arms over her chest. Clearly she wanted a fight.

I didn't. Quickly, I filled her in on the high points of my recent life of crime detection, including having my head used for batting practice. I omitted from my report Eliane's opinion of what Martin wanted with Laura. No point in unduly alarming Liz.

"Those bastards!" she said, transferring her belligerence to Theo and Martin. Good. "And Laura? You said she's safe but —"

"Don't ask because I'm not going to tell you. You'll have to trust me."

"Hmmph," she grunted. "So what do you plan to do?"

I shrugged. "Find Theo and Martin. Have a chat with them. Make them go away. That's what you're paying me for, right?"

"Well, yeah, but . . . hell, don't you want someone to go with you?"

I shook my head. "Nah. Now that I know what kind of scum I'm dealing with, I'll go prepared."

"With what?" Liz scoffed. "An Uzi?"

"Not exactly," I said, thinking of my .357 Smith and Wesson's irresistible voice of reason. "Just a reliable friend."

"When it's over, you'll let me know? Right away?"

"Right away," I assured her. "I'm sure Laura will be eager to see you."

She broke into a goofy smile at that and I let myself out, admiring the pansies and the very, very young pansy-packer. Ah well.

The Blalock residence was in a development of homes built in the sixties and seventies — split-level houses with natural wood siding and brick trim, two-car garages, big decks above the garage, lots and lots of trees. Nice, comfortable California-inspired structures. Elizabeth Blalock's home was on Seaview Terrace, and while I couldn't exactly see the ocean through the madrones, I had no doubt it was there. A blue 1988 Chrysler Le Baron sat in the driveway, so presumably Mrs. Blalock was at home. I parked on the street and walked up a flagstone path bordered with ranunculi and Iceland poppies. Very pretty. Too pretty to be the place where Martin Fell had hatched his sick schemes.

Elizabeth Blalock answered my knock at once, and with a start I realized that she was not much older than I. She, however, had convinced herself that her life was on the wane. Her once dark hair was streaked with gray, and though she stood straight and tall, I could tell it was with an effort. Her face bore the wrinkles of an old woman's, and eyes which should have been snapping brown were vague and faded. Life had clearly not been easy. Everything about her shouted that after a long struggle she had finally bowed to adversity. After all, being mother to Theo and aunt to Martin would have been heavy burdens for anyone. And then to lose her husband? Bad luck.

"Mrs. Blalock?" I inquired, deliberately not proferring my card.

She clutched her cardigan to her throat with hands that already bore age spots. "Yes." Her eyes were wary, traveling past me to the street and back again.

"I'm Caitlin Reece, a private investigator. If you have a few moments, I'd like to ask you some questions about your nephew, Martin."

Her lips compressed into a thin line. "Is he in trouble again?" She shook her head. "I just hope he doesn't drag Theo into it."

Sensing an opening, I decided to go for broke. "Yes, Martin is in trouble. But with your help, maybe we can get Theo out of it before things get too bad."

She looked at me, a tiny gleam of hope in her eyes, and I felt like a heel. Get Theo out of it indeed. The little turd had thwacked me on the head. I was going to nail his ass with an assault charge. "Well, all right," she said. "Please come in. I was just going to make coffee. Would you like some?"

"I'd love some," I said as she led me through an entry hall into a bright and cheery kitchen painted yellow and white. I took a seat at a little kitchen table in a nook that looked out on a backyard rose garden.

"Theo's father and I thought we'd heard the last of Martin when he went away to prison eight years ago," she said. "That was wishful thinking, I guess. He just keeps turning up. Like a bad penny." She put two big blue ceramic mugs of coffee on the table, a couple of spoons, a sugar bowl, and a pint of half-and-half.

"Oh?" I remarked, fixing my coffee. "Has he turned up recently?"

"He came to the door just after my husband died last year. In August. Connor had a heart attack," Elizabeth explained. I nodded, for form's sake. "Well, I just stood there. I was that surprised. He'd grown up, of course. When he went away to prison he was just a boy. Seventeen. Now he's a man." The thought clearly disturbed her because she stirred her coffee vigorously, unnecessarily. "I thought he was going to ask for money, but he didn't. Then I thought he might have come to offer condolences on his uncle's death. But he didn't do that, either. What he wanted was, well, his things."

"His things?"

"Yes. The things he'd left in his room. Books, papers, notebooks, clothes — those kinds of things. Well, Connor had packed them all up and put them in the attic when it became obvious Martin wasn't coming back here. But for some reason, I didn't want to tell him we still had them. I didn't want to let him in the house, you see," she explained. "He frightened me. Even with Eileen and Shannon here. So I lied and said we'd sent everything off to Goodwill."

"Did he believe you?"

She shrugged. "I guess so. I haven't seen him since. But I can tell you he got pretty angry — his face turned red and he started to stammer — just like he did when he was a kid. The thought went through my mind that if my sister hadn't been here he might have, well, struck me. He was that angry."

"Is the stuff still in the attic?" I asked, hardly daring to hope.

"I suppose so," she said. "I didn't bother to look, but I suppose so. Eileen and Shannon were helping me pack up Connor's things and they were in and out of the attic, but I don't think they threw anything out."

"Can I take a look at it?" I asked.

"Oh, I don't know . . ." she said, vaguely. "Do you really have to? Things are in such a jumble up there."

"It might be helpful," I insisted gently.

She crossed her arms, clutching herself, looking out the window at the roses.

"Beautiful garden" I told her. "That big cream-colored rose with the pink center, isn't that a Peace?"

She looked back with a shy smile. "Yes. Do you like roses?"

"Love them. But I have a black thumb. I wouldn't dare plant any."

She laughed and I saw some of the tension go out of her. "What's Martin done now?" she asked.

"Assault," I said, rearranging the facts a little. "That alone should get him sent back to prison."

"Really? Do you really think so?" Her eagerness was pathetic.

"Yes, I do. But I have to find him first."

"Are you working for the person he assaulted? Is that why you want to find him?"

"Not exactly. The assault came in the course of my investigating something else."

"What?"

"Oh, something off-the-wall," I said, trying to downplay the photos. No need to scare her half to death. "It wasn't a crime, but it upset my client a lot."

"Photos," she said in a weak voice. "He sent chopped-up photos, didn't he?"

"Yeah, he did."

She compressed her lips again and looked out to the rose garden. I decided to say nothing. She was right on the edge and I didn't want to push anymore. If she wanted to help me, she would. "I haven't thought about those in years," she said, turning back to me. "That's how he was caught, you know."

"I know. I read his file."

She exhaled audibly. "I was so upset when his mother asked us to take him. Even though the insurance money paid to send him to Glenlion Academy. He just wasn't a Glenlion kind of boy. Not like Theo," she said with a mixture of pride and regret. "Poor Theo. He was a nice, sweet boy, a good boy, good manners, good, solid grades, no discipline problems. Then Martin came to live with us. And

Martin ruined him the way he ruined everything he touched."

I decided to just let her talk.

"Martin was two years older than Theo. They were born on the same day — Christmas Day. Theo thought this was terrific, that he had a 'star twin.' That's what Martin called him. I never did get along with my brother when we were kids and as adults we just never visited. So the two boys hadn't seen much of each other growing up. But once Martin came to live with us, Theo took right to him. Idolized him. Martin was smart, so smart . . . and Theo could never think of a reason to say no to him. He had some kind of hold over Theo." She shook her head. "I never understood it."

"Why did you agree to let Martin come here?" I asked.

She shook her head. "Maude, Martin's mom, was so devastated when my brother was killed that I said yes out of pity. She asked and asked me. I finally just . . . gave in."

She seemed to shake herself a little. "Those were black days," she said. "I really don't want to dwell on them. If you want to look through Martin's things, they're in the attic. I'm afraid you may get dirty," she apologized.

"No problem," I assured her.

She led me down the hall to the bedroom wing and reached up to pull down a folding staircase. "There's a light on the wall just to your right," she said. "I haven't been up here in a while, but Martin's things were in a couple of large cartons over by the window. My husband packed them. He marked them with Martin's name. Take as long as you like."

I climbed the stairs, located the light switch, and navigated my way through stacks of small liquor cartons, several battered blue metal trunks, a couple of upright cardboard wardrobes, a stack of items wrapped in green garbage bags, a couple of mirrors, and the usual litter of skis, tennis rackets, and golf clubs. Without much trouble, I found the stack of five boxes marked MARTIN and, clearing a space in front of the window, sat down with one of the cartons beside me. The tape holding the box shut was yellowed and brittle and yielded easily to my Swiss army knife. Unfolding the flaps gingerly, I looked inside. I'm not sure what I expected but the jumble of books, tapes, magazines, and notebooks was a definite anticlimax. I decided I'd better open all the boxes then decide what to spend my time looking at. Elizabeth wouldn't be too happy with my taking all day up here.

I hauled the other four boxes over, slit them open and stirred the contents around. They seemed to be mostly clothes and shoes. I wondered if the two big brown suitcases were Martin's, too. On the off chance that they were, I pulled them over and unzipped them. Big deal. School uniforms, rugby shorts and shirts, running shoes, some ribbons for track.

In a pocket of one suitcase I found a copy of Glenlion's 1985 literary magazine called *The Ikon.* Obviously Martin had kept it for a reason. A nice glossy magazine with a stitched cover, it looked classy. Obviously some of those outrageous private school fees had gone into the production. I flipped the pages quickly and realized with a shock of surprise that Martin Fell's writing comprised a good third of the magazine. He had a rather long and derivative short story about a boy who went to sleep and woke up as an alien. Alas, nobody could tell. Goodness, another Kafka fan. There were half a dozen poems filled with the usual adolescent angst which I quickly passed over, and three which were stylistically pretty good. Their subject matter, however, was very unsettling. One was a conversation with a corpse, one was final thoughts of a suicide, and the last was the interior monologue of, I guessed, a murderer. Strong stuff for a high-school magazine. I put *The Ikon* on the floor and zipped the suitcases shut. That left only the box of books and notebooks.

I dumped the contents out onto the floor, raising a cloud of dust which made me sneeze. Out tumbled paperback copies of H.P. Lovecraft, A.A. Merritt, H.G. Wells, a well-thumbed volume of Bram Stoker's *Dracula,* some books on black magic and satanism, *The Dictionary of Imaginary Places,* some Stephen King novels, a book by Clive Barker, and a collection of Ramsay Campbell's short stories. Obviously young Martin liked horror and the macabre. However, the notebooks interested me most. If he fancied himself a writer, it was possible that these books contained his drafts. I opened one — a fat spiral-bound notebook with a black cover. Inside was written what I recognized as one of Caliban's complaints from *The Tempest:*

Sometimes am I
All wound with adders who with cloven tongues
Do hiss me into madness.

Interesting. Did young Martin see himself as Caliban, the misshapen monster? I flipped through the first of the notebooks and sure enough, there were two drafts of his *Ikon* story, "The Possession," and several versions of each of the *Ikon* poems as well as workings and reworkings of unpublished poems. The two other spiral-bound notebooks were likewise filled with Martin's poetry and prose. I piled these on top of the literary magazine to take away with me.

Under the black notebooks was a photo album. The back of my neck prickled as I lifted the album to the light, brushing the dust off the cover. I opened it. The first page contained nothing but snapshots of Theo, Laura, the school, the ocean — that kind of thing. Camouflage? I guessed so, because the very next page contained Martin's early efforts at weird photo collages. A middle-aged woman (one of his teachers?) was depicted first at the chalkboard, then with the head of a dog, next with the body of a pig, and last, disappearing into the maw of an alligator. Various other adults had received the same treatment. On the fourth page, Martin had turned his efforts to girls. Photos, presumably of his classmates, featured girls with cats' bodies and cats with girls' heads. But he must have found all this pretty repetitive because on the next page he had begun one of his human-body-parts collages, which I recognized from the photos he had sent Laura. I examined this one with particular interest. Stuck in the fold of the pages were a score of unmounted photos — pictures of a handsome, middle-aged woman with various family members at birthdays, a garden party, Christmas, swimming, and just sitting reading. Several of these photos had been enlarged and duplicated and three of them had pieces cut out of them — a head with a ski mask, a bikinied torso, bare arms and legs, minus hands and feet. All these were loose between the pages. Also loose was a five-by-eight photo of a bed which, I supposed, was going to be the background for this artistic effort. I didn't want to even guess what the final product might have depicted. Swallowing, I poked the arms and legs gingerly with one finger. Then I saw, wedged in the fold of the book, a slip of buff-colored paper. Grasping it gently, I eased it out. And almost yelled aloud in delight. IVERSON'S PHOTOS, it said, with an address and phone number. Goddamn! The place was still in business — I passed it every time I went to British Fish 'N Chips.

Closing the photo album, I placed it on the bottom of the stack I intended to carry away. Then I straightened up, stretching. There seemed to be nothing else of Martin's here. I restacked the boxes, re-piled the suitcases, took one final look around, and saw, far in a back corner of the attic, another brown suitcase, a smaller version of the ones that held Martin's belongings. Slowly, I made my way through boxes and over skis to the corner of the attic, hefted the suitcase, which was very light, and brought it back to the window. With a sense of dread, I unzipped the suitcase only to find a long, flat box, a gift box, that bore the yellow and white logo of The Bay, a national department store. What? Even more bizarre, the box had a big yellow ribbon tied around it. I lifted the box out of the suitcase, slipped off the ribbon, and gingerly pried up the lid, half expecting wildlife to scamper out. But none did. Setting the lid down gently, I bent to see the treasure Martin had so lovingly preserved. Whatever it was, it was further wrapped in white tissue, and I carefully peeled back the paper. Inside, in separate Ziploc bags were three pairs of women's underwear and a pair of red bikini bathing suit bottoms. Suddenly I felt faint. Sitting down heavily, I put my head between my knees.

When I was sure I wouldn't pass out, I looked at the box again. Why had this affected me so much, this final proof of Martin's culpability? Eliane was right. Photos and panties. Goddamnit, she was right. I closed my eyes. How did someone get from reading Shakespeare to . . . this? What had happened? God knew that I, too, had read *The Tempest* and most of the books that had tumbled out of that cardboard box. But I ended up as a Crown Prosecutor while Fell had descended into what? Madness? No way. I completely rejected that. He might have six or eight major screws loose, but no way was he legally insane. This guy was *compos mentis*. But skewed. Twisted. I wished Eliane were here so I could have asked her how this kind of thing happens and why the pattern is so damned predictable.

But then I realized, she wouldn't care. Answering the question why was not of primary importance to her. And maybe not even of secondary importance.

Identifying the behavior and flagging it for law enforcement personnel — that was her interest. And that was the difference between us. I wanted very much to know why; Eliane couldn't care less.

I put the lid back on the box from The Bay, piled the other stuff on top of it, hefted the load, and navigated my way toward the stairs.

Elizabeth heard me coming and met me in the hall. "Did you find anything useful?" she asked hopefully.

"Maybe," I said. "I've only had a chance to glance at this stuff. Do you mind if I take it away where I can spend some time studying it?"

She waved a hand dismissively. "I wish you'd take it all. Well, not you, but I wish someone would."

On my way to the front door, I noticed a framed photo of a man and a boy in yellow oilskins aboard what looked to be a working fishing boat, the man's arm around the boy.

Seeing my interest, Elizabeth said: "Connor and Theo on Con's trawler. Theo loved to go out with the salmon fleet and sometimes, on school holidays, Con let him. Of course once Martin came, all that changed."

"Do you still have any of Theo's things?" I asked her.

She shook her head. "No. After Martin . . . went away, Theo became moody and difficult. He didn't even graduate," she said bitterly. "He stopped seeing that nice girlfriend of his and moved out as soon as he could. He took all his things. We don't hear from him." There was a volume of tragedy behind that statement.

I wondered if Elizabeth knew that Theo had eventually married that nice girlfriend. I guessed not. Well, she was certainly right about one thing — Martin did indeed seem to spoil what he touched. His own family, and his cousin Theo's family, too. I wondered fleetingly about the accidents both fathers had suffered — Martin's father a logging accident and Theo's a heart attack. Seemed pretty coincidental. But I really didn't see how they could be attributed to Martin. Or could they? After all, Caliban had hated Prospero, his master and father stand-in. Hmmm . . .

"One last thing," I asked Elizabeth. "Did Martin act in a Shakespearean play at school the year he was living with you?"

She smiled sadly. "Oh yes. And so did Theo. *The Tempest,* it was. Theo was Ariel. Martin was Caliban. Fitting, don't you think?"

"Was Theo's girlfriend in the play too?"

Elizabeth nodded. "Yes. She was Miranda, Prospero's daughter."

Curiouser and curiouser. "Thanks. You've been more than kind."

She held the door open for me. "You will try . . . to help Theo if you can, won't you?" I nodded. "And Martin. Would you let me know . . . if he goes back to prison? I'd like to know that."

"I will," I promised.

I stuffed my load into the back seat of the MG, U-turned, and drove back to Oak Bay. All this had been very interesting but I was no whit closer to finding where the two of them were holed up. Elizabeth was clearly so out of touch with her son that she no longer even knew him. No joy there.

At the local McDonald's, I ordered a chocolate shake and fish sandwich and ate as I drove past the golf course toward the marina. On impulse, I pulled into the public parking lot just north of the marina and parked as close to the steep bank as I could get. Then I sat, finishing my milkshake, staring out to sea.

I needed to pull something together soon. Laura couldn't stay at Gray's forever. Martin and Theo weren't going to hide forever. I needed to find them. Wrap this thing up so Laura and Liz, separately or together, could get on with the rest of their lives. And Eliane? What was my obligation to her? I had never formally agreed to work for her, but I had as much as promised her that when I found Martin, I would let her talk to him. Well, that could be arranged. Once he was in custody, I didn't see that an interview couldn't be arranged. Only this time, I'd keep bars between them if I were she. And what about Theo? Could I really keep him out of things, as I'd told his mother I would? I really didn't think so. After all, he, not Martin, was most likely the one who had clobbered me. An assault charge would stick to them equally. Nope. Theo was most likely going to serve time, too. I couldn't summon up any regrets. What the hell was he thinking of, letting Martin scare the daylights out of Laura with those weird photos?

I rolled down my window and tossed the remains of my fish sandwich bun to a particularly bold seagull who was patrolling the parking lot. Today the sky was achingly, flawlessly blue, the ocean indigo. Out on the water half a dozen sailboats were scudding along, their sails white and full, creamy wakes foaming behind them. The seagull hopped up onto the hood of my MG and, fixing me with the unblinking gaze of one shoe-button eye, rasped a request for more lunch. That ended my reverie.

"No deal," I told him. "Gotta go. Move it, razor-beak." I started the engine and the bird took one ungainly hop to the pavement where he eyed me reproachfully, awaiting another diner.

At Iverson's Photos, on Foul Bay Road, an artsy-looking young fellow with flowing tresses, a T-shirt with a whale on it that said, WHALES, SAVE US! and baggy black cotton pants, listened to my story suspiciously.

"Can't do it," he informed me. "If they were your photos, that would be one thing, but they aren't."

"But Martin can't get in until Friday and he was so looking forward to seeing them." I pouted.

He shook his head firmly. "Sorry. No can do."

I drummed my fingers on the glass countertop, thinking of telling the obstreperous youth that national security was at stake or the honor of womankind, but he had a prematurely jaded look about him that discouraged further invention on my part. What the hell — there was always breaking and entering. I didn't want the damned photos anyhow, just Fell's address.

Back at home, I had hardly closed the front door when Lester charged me. "I've got it!" he declared, waving what looked like an invoice. "Theo's boat. I've got it!"

"So?" I asked, depositing my load of Fell's belongings on the sofa and tossing my bomber jacket at the coat tree. I was, I admit, a tad testy. Failure does that to me. "We know his dad left him an out-of-commission trawler. Big deal."

He shoved the invoice under my nose. "Drydock fees."

"Drydock, shmrydock. So what?" I waved the invoice aside.

"Live-aboard fees," he said patiently. "Prepaid through June."

"What?" I grabbed the invoice. "Why didn't you say so." At the top of the invoice was clearly printed the name of the shipyard — Carlson's Marina and Drydock. And Theo Blalock's signature was on it. "Where is this place?"

"Esquimalt," he said. "Out towards Sooke. I've already called."

And then it hit me. "This is all very nice," I told him, "but we don't know the name of the damned boat."

He looked at me in horror. "We don't, do we?"

"No shit, Sherlock. And we can't exactly wander around asking questions."

"But —"

"Think about it. We'd spook them for sure. Both of them know what I look like."

"But they don't know what *I* look like," he said.

I knew where this was leading. "Oh, no. Absolutely not."

"Why not? How dangerous can asking questions get?"

I cackled a derisive laugh.

"All right, all right, I take that back. But I'd be super careful."

"Let me mull it over," I said. "No promises." Seeing his distress, I ruffled his hair. "I'm going to rest my eyes for a half-hour. You keep thinking."

In my bathroom, I took two aspirins, splashed water on my face, and hoped that twenty minutes or so of shut-eye would eliminate this spacey feeling of being not here. This seemed to me to be a drama in which I was acting a part or, as I had felt so vividly earlier, a dream. I kicked off my shoes, lay down on my bed, wrapped myself in my quilt, closed my eyes . . . and was immediately, or so I fancied, awakened by Lester.

"Caitlin," he whispered urgently from the doorway, "I've got it!"

I cracked an eye open. "You're going to have knobs on your head if this isn't important."

"I've got the name of the boat — the *Sea Queen*!" he said in an excited whisper.

"The what?"

"The boat. The trawler. Theo's boat!"

Tossing the quilt off my legs, I sat up. "I hear you." With a growing sense of panic I looked at my watch — I had snoozed away the entire afternoon. "Why in hell didn't you wake me up?"

"Er, well, I've been busy. I made a few phone calls that didn't pan out and then I got the bright idea to go back and talk to Renata — you know, the landlord at Theo's apartment. She didn't know anything. But her kid sure did."

"What? Ajay? He can hardly talk."

"I know. But he had to show me that toy car of

his again and what with his jabbering about it I could hardly talk to his mom. So I asked her what was so important about the damned car. Guess what she said."

"Tell me."

"Theo gave it to Ajay. And it's a *boat,* not a car."

"Jesus. 'Tio see weenie.' Theo's *Sea Queen*. Out of the mouths of babes." I jammed my feet into my Reeboks and headed for the closet. "Grab a warm jacket, junior. And some gloves. You're going to be doing the detective's second least favorite job."

"Oh yeah?" he asked as I threaded my belt through the holster for my Smith and Wesson .357 Magnum, then fed it back through the loops in my jeans. It made a reassuring bulge in the small of my back. "What's that?"

"Surveillance."

"Okay," he said, eyes bright. We were in the front hall before it hit him. "Wait. You said me. What are you going to be doing?"

"Meeting Ariel and Caliban."

Although Lester fretted, I drove my MG to Esquimalt. I was much too antsy to sit still in the passenger's seat of Lester's Samurai. We took the coast road to Sooke and as we came down off a little rise and headed for the ocean, I saw that the beautiful spring day had vanished as I slept. A westerly wind had blown a storm front in, and in the eerie twilight the thunderheads were purple against a pewter sky. Out to sea, greasy-looking black breakers rolled and surged, tumbling into foam as waves were driven onto the rocky shore. It was going to be a wild night at Carlson's.

"Warm enough?' I asked Lester, hoping he was because this was one of the days when my MG's on-again off-again heater was off.

"Sure," he replied manfully. "I've got my down parka on, see?"

"Good fellow."

The road curved inland just a little, away from the sea, and through the pines and madrones that separated us from the coast, I could see the masts of sailboats, a long wooden dock, and a weathered wood boathouse. Carlson's Marina, no doubt. "We'll carry on up the road," I told Lester. "See if there's a convenience store, a corner market, something like that. Maybe they shop there."

Around the next bend, a ramshackle collection of structures attested to the presence of civilization. Two partly dismantled cars nestled side by side under the roof of a corrugated tin shack; a pair of gas pumps stood sentinel on the tarmac; and just beyond the pumps, a once-white, dilapidated one-story structure bore the unlikely name of the Koastal Kwik-Mart. I guessed it was worth a try. Tossing Lester ten bucks, I got out of the MG and stretched. "You fill the tank. I'll chat up the help."

The flimsy front door of the Kwik-Mart snapped shut on my heels, startling the skinny teenage girl at the cash register.

"God DAMN!" she said, addressing her fingernails, which she was busily painting the color of ripe Bing cherries. She gave me a reproachful look, blew deliberately on her nails, and went back to the business at hand, so to speak. A bored-looking kid with bad skin, lank brown hair that needed washing, and a voluminous black sweatshirt, she was not exactly the Kwik-Mart's most effective marketing tool. In fact, customer relations was clearly a language she did not speak. Ignoring her, I whistled cheerily, meandering among the shelves, casually gathering up a load of candy bars, potato chips, dip, a package of cheese crackers, and a six-pack of Cokes. I wandered a little more, then brought my purchases to the checkout counter and plunked them down. The kid sighed a sigh that came all the way from her stylishly unlaced high-tops and began using one enameled nail to peck the prices into the cash register.

"Kinda quiet around here," I remarked.

She looked at me as if I had just beamed down from a distant planet. Ah, the arrogance of youth.

"Q.E.D., eh?"

"What?" she deigned to inquire, interrupting her pecking to cast me a world-weary look.

"Q.E.D. *Quod erat demonstrandum.* A legal term nowadays but one which was originally applied to mathematical concepts. Often used to indicate things which are self-evident."

She gave me a sidelong look. Her eyes were hazel and, I realized, quite pretty. "Do you, like, want something else? We close in about ten minutes."

"Me?" I asked ingenuously. "Nope. Just these chips and things. I'm on my way to the marina to join my friends. We're going to party out the storm."

"Your friends?" she said incredulously, pecking finger poised above the cash register keys. "The twins? Those guys on the *Sea Queen*?"

Well, that was easy. "Hey," I said, in feigned admiration for her powers of deduction. "How'd you guess?"

"They're the only live-aboards Carlson has right now," she said smugly. "They buy stuff here. Are they really friends of yours?"

"Mmmhmm," I replied in elaborate disinterest, perusing the latest copy of *Soap Opera Digest.*

"Cool," she opined. "They're like, rilly weird, aren't they?"

"Uh huh." *Rilly?*

"But nice weird, if you know what I mean. Especially Martin."

Oh yeah, he's nice all right. Rilly nice. "Mmmhmm."

"Okay, that'll be thirteen fifty-four," she said. I handed her a twenty and she made change laboriously. "Tell them Corrie said hi, okay?" She tossed my purchases into a cardboard box and slid them down the counter to me. "Sorry for the box, but we're, like, recycling."

At that moment, Lester came in, giving me an opportunity to escape. I carried the box out to the MG, re-packed it a little, and put it in the back. Then I leaned against the car in the blustery twilight and tried to think. It was about six o'clock — the Kwik Mart would be closing soon. With any luck, I could get away with what I had planned. I took a deep breath, trying to calm my racing heart.

Lester joined me, his eyebrows raised in a question. I motioned him inside the car.

"Okay, this is what we'll do. We'll drive down to the marina, see if there's anyone in the office, and ask where the *Sea Queen* is located."

"If there isn't anyone in the office?"

"Then we go to Plan B."

Lester groaned. "Tell me more about Plan A."

"Atta boy — we may as well be optimistic, right? Okay, here's the deal. We drive into the marina, park, and once we find out where the *Sea Queen* is located, you deliver that box of goodies. Tell them it's a present from Corrie. At the Kwik Mart."

He swallowed nervously, adjusting his glasses.

"Then you come back and let me know what you've seen. Ways in, large objects I might fall over in the dark, that sort of thing. Okay?"

"Okay. And then?"

I shrugged. "Then I go in and get Theo and Martin."

He looked at me worriedly.

I punched him in the shoulder. "It'll be fine. C'mon. Let's visit the marina office."

As we pulled away from the Kwik Mart, he asked, "By the way, what *is* Plan B?"

"Don't ask," I told him. "It involves breaking and entering and other illegal acts."

He sank down into his parka and didn't say a word.

As luck would have it, there was only one car in the marina parking lot — Theo's black Cherokee. Lester and I crunched across the gravel parking lot to the office — a cedar-shingled wooden structure I could barely make out in the gloom. Of course it was closed and locked. Fortunately, not very well. I rattled the doorknob, crouched down to examine it with my penlight, slipped a credit card between door and frame, and had the door open in a jiffy.

"Stay in the car," I told Lester. "Honk if anyone comes up the walk."

Inside, I used my light sparingly. On the wall just inside the door was a huge plastic-covered map of the marina, showing the various wharves and slips for seaworthy craft and the boatyard section for craft under repair. No fancy filing system here. No sirree. The names of boat owners were simply written directly on the plastic in the appropriate slips. I counted over a hundred boats berthed in the marina, but only four in drydock. And, if I could believe Corrie, Theo and Martin were the only live-aboards. The way to the boatyard was simple — around the office, onto the main dock, straight ahead past all the sailboats and motorboats, and then left onto a narrower dock which led back to dry land again. BLALOCK was written in the first spot to the right of the dock.

I snapped my light off, closed the office door behind me, and loped to my car. Time to send Lester on his way.

"No heroics, okay?" I told him as I explained where the *Sea Queen* was located and handed him the box of goodies. "Just play delivery boy."

"Right. I'm a friend of Corrie's. I've thought it all through."

"Yeah, that'll do. Be agreeable and dense. Smile a lot. And be sure to tell them someone's waiting for you in the car."

"Okay." He hefted the box, clearly anxious to be off. I wondered when he'd stopped listening.

Grabbing him by one ear, I said, "Earth to Lester."

"Ow," he said, looking at me in surprise.

"Be careful, guy. Toss the box and run like hell if you have to. Got that?"

He nodded.

I patted his cheek.

"Now get going."

I drove my MG out of the parking lot and hid it in a stand of cedar shrubs I'd noticed, partway up a little path just off the rutted main road leading to the marina. It was now fully dark. I could hear the crash of waves on the rocks and, as I hurried back through the parking lot, the creak of wood rubbing on ropes and hulls as boats stirred restlessly in their slips. The dock surged beneath my feet like a live thing as I staggered past the office in search of a big Bayliner I had spotted earlier. When I thought I'd come far enough along the dock, I snapped my light on. Yup. There she was — a fifty-footer, with a flying bridge, a nice overhang sheltering the door down into the cabin, and the improbable name *Instead.* I crouched on the slippery boards of the dock and, as the surge sent the Bayliner my way, I jumped aboard. Tucking myself into the overhang, I hunkered down, waiting for Lester. He'd have to pass *Instead* on the way back to the parking lot. It would be impossible to miss him.

It seemed that I'd hardly settled down to wait when I heard the sound of running feet on the boards of the dock. Peering out of the Bayliner's companionway, over the bulk of the cabin, I saw a black silhouette against the lighter charcoal gray of the sky. As it pounded past me, I recognized the runner. It was Lester.

"Ssst, Lester!" I called softly. "Over here. In the boat." I turned my penlight on so he could see where I was.

"Caitlin!" he called, stumbling and falling to one knee on the dock. "Oh, my God!"

I vaulted onto the dock beside him, my heart hammering against my ribs. "Are you hurt? What is it?"

"In the trunk," he blubbered. "There's someone in the trunk! There was blood on it, Caitlin. I put my hand on it to try to open it and it came away all sticky with blood."

"It'll wash off," I told him roughly, wrestling him onto the Bayliner and sitting him against the cabin door. "Now what in hell happened? What trunk?"

He took a couple of deep breaths. "Okay. I went down the dock, just like you said. I found the path leading to the drydocked boats. I found the *Sea Queen*. Just before I got there, I heard this thumping sound. I looked around. It was pretty dark but I could see there was a kind of road, hardly more than a couple of tire tracks behind the drydocked boats. The thumping sound was coming from some bushes by that road. I set the box down and went over there." He paused. "There was —

there is — a big black car in the bushes. The thumping sound was coming from the trunk. I put my hand on it but it was locked. I said 'Is someone in there?' and the thumping started again. I said 'Are you hurt?' and they thumped more. Jesus, Caitlin. Who is it? Did Martin and Theo do this?"

"I don't know," I told him. "Listen up. Here's what we're going to do. There's a phone in the office back there. Break the window to get in. Call the cops. Call an ambulance. Wait for them."

"Me? What about you?" he squeaked. "You're not going out there, are you? Why not wait for the police?"

"I have to," I told him. "I've got a very bad feeling about this, junior. And if I wait, and I'm too late, I'm going to spend a lot of days and nights in regret. Now come on." He didn't move. "Lester," I said softly. "I'm counting on you. Whoever's in that trunk is counting on you. Let's go do what we have to do." I held my hand out to him and, to my great relief, he took it. I helped him off the Bayliner and sent him in the direction of the office. Then, with a sinking feeling in my gut, I set off down the dock the other way.

As I padded through the forest of bare masts, that godawful spacey feeling came over me again and for a minute I seemed to be wandering in a forest, among pale trees whose bare branches were raised in supplication to some wintertime deity. I shook my head to clear it and was back on the dock again. Boats moaned and strained against their lashings, *thunk*ing now and then as the growing swell tossed them against the wooden pilings. Loose lines and sheets made gunshot snaps in the wind and an empty gallon-sized plastic water container went bouncing down the dock like a gleeful imp on an errand.

I found the little gravel path that led to the drydocked boats and with relief, stepped onto solid ground. Ahead of me loomed the bulk of a trawler, yellow light showing through one of her portholes. The *Sea Queen,* I guessed. I navigated a course to the left of her, trying to follow Lester's directions, trying to be careful, trying to be quiet. But even stopping every few paces to look and listen, I still managed to fall over the cardboard box of goodies. As I lay on the ground, cursing, fumbling for my penlight, the moon sailed out of a ragged scrap of clouds, turning clumps of darkness to low-growing shrubs and showing me, dead ahead, the silver and black shape of an automobile. I swallowed and rolled to my knees, brushing gravel off my hands. Four paces took me over to the car and I knelt behind it, touching with one finger a sticky handprint on the trunk. I looked down at the license plate. As I had feared it would, it read ST CYR. This was Eliane's car. The car I had ridden in. With her. I laid my head against the cold metal, looking up at the moon, praying that this was a dream from which I would momentarily awaken. But of course, it wasn't.

I reached in my pocket for my lockpicks.

Chapter 13

Penlight in one hand, pick in the other, I popped the trunk lock after far too many minutes of silent swearing. I jammed my picks back in my pocket and shone the penlight into the dark maw of the trunk. It revealed only a shapeless, dark mass that I quickly realized was a body wrapped in a dark-colored wool blanket. Shoving the penlight between my teeth, I grabbed the first body part I could, shook it, then fumbled for the blanket's edge. It was securely taped and I picked at the tape until I got a good strip started, then ripped it loose, unwrapping the blanket as I went. This revealed the body's head. A woman's head. I smoothed the hair off the face . . . and cried aloud. I knew that face. It was Romany, Eliane's young assistant. Her eyes were closed, her mouth taped shut, and as far as I could tell, she wasn't breathing. I had to get her out of the trunk. Taking two fistfuls of the blanket, I sat her up, hoisted her over my shoulder, and staggered as far into the bushes as I could. Letting her down none too gently, I tore the tape off her mouth, stretched her out, and started CPR. "C'mon, c'mon," I muttered, doing the task mechanically, trying not to think about what the hell Romany was doing here. After what seemed a year, she gave a little sigh and started breathing for herself. She did not, however, open her eyes. No wonder. A gash on the side of her head was sticky with blood. I thought I knew whose handiwork that was. Someone who loved to clobber women.

Picking her up, I carried her to the car and put her on the back seat. I wrapped her in the blanket I had torn off her, checked her breathing, then realized there was nothing more I could do for her. Lester would lead the cops to Romany. As for me, I had business with Fell and Blalock on the trawler. And more than one score to settle. I brushed the silly crimson hair out of Romany's eyes and wiped my bloodied hands on my jeans.

The *Sea Queen,* a rather small trawler, sat in a pair of canvas and chain slings. The slings were attached to a crane and the whole apparatus held the *Sea Queen* about six feet off the ground, leaving all parts of it accessible for repairs. A wooden scaffolding had been erected on the far side of the trawler and a makeshift stairway without rails hugged the craft's near side. I guessed that living aboard a craft under repairs was not exactly within the letter of the law, but evidently Carlson had been amenable to persuasion.

I put one hand on the rickety stairway and winced as it moved. Still, I had to climb it. Taking a deep breath, I went up on all fours. Heights make me giddy, so I was very glad indeed to step onto the trawler's deck and scuttle into the shadow of the wheelhouse. The moon made things far too bright, I thought, as I cautiously stood up and looked around for some way to descend to the trawler's hold. My knowledge of boats is almost nonexistent, but I knew enough to realize that there had to be a cabin around here somewhere. Forward, I guessed. Sure enough, a little flight of metal stairs led down to an open stairwell. A door, at present closed, presumably led into the cabin. I descended the stairs cautiously, and stood outside the door. I touched my .357 once for reassurance, made sure I could draw it easily if I needed to, then wrenched the door open, and burst inside.

It took my brain a couple of moments to make sense of what my eyes were seeing. Two young men, dressed similarly in jeans and black T-shirts, dark hair combed back from their foreheads, stood facing me. They looked somewhat alike, but they were far from being twins, as Corrie had asserted.

One, the closest to me, was a small guy, maybe my size, with a pleasant rosy-cheeked face, blue eyes, and curly dark hair. He had a weak mouth and chin, however, and that mouth was now set in disapproval. In fact, his whole affect was that of distress. Theo Blalock, I guessed.

It was the other man, however, who arrested my attention. I had seen this face before. My size, but slighter, this man was thin-faced and pale with straight dark hair combed back from a widow's peak and bright, manic, anthracite eyes. He smiled a goblin's smile, full of secret glee. Oh yes, I had seen this face before — the morning I'd been clobbered outside Blalock's apartment. No one needed to tell me this was Martin Fell, Theo's cousin and role model, his "star twin," his *doppelganger.*

Between them knelt a woman, hands tied in front of her, white shirt ripped open, a livid bruise on the side of her face. Fell had one hand wound in the woman's unbound hair and, as if he had arranged this *tableau* especially for me, he pulled her head cruelly back, displaying his prize. My heart seemed to stop — the woman on the floor was Eliane St. Cyr. Fell held a fish scaling knife to Eliane's throat, and I saw with dismay that he and Theo were struggling for it.

An instant of hot, red rage made my ears ring and I prayed for ice, for control, for the shrewdness and cunning I would need to bring Eliane out of this alive. Because some part of me had decided, in the moment I saw Fell display her to me like a hunting trophy, that I would settle for nothing less. He would not kill her. I would not permit it.

"I thought you might come," Fell said to me.

As if he realized that further opposition was futile, Theo stepped away. Fell smiled at his cousin, took a firmer grip on Eliane's hair and hauled her to her feet. The instant he took his eyes off me, I drew my .357.

But he had anticipated me. With a chuckle, Fell hugged Eliane in a ghastly parody of intimacy, one hand inside her shirt, clasping her to him, the other hand holding the knife to her throat, using her body to shield his.

"Oh no, not quite yet," he told me.

"Martin," Theo pleaded, stepping back toward his cousin.

Fell pressed the knife harder against Eliane's throat and I saw a line of blood where the blade cut her flesh. Tears ran down her face but she did not flinch or cry out.

"Get out of here, Blalock," I told him. "There's nothing you can do."

"I . . . I . . ." he stammered, but neither Fell nor I were listening to him. Finally his nerve broke and I heard him fumbling with the door, running up the steps onto the deck, then crashing down the wooden staircase at the side of the trawler.

"Well, *he's* in a hurry to meet his maker," Fell remarked. But he never took his eyes from me. Look away, dammit, look away, I willed. Just give me one moment of inattention.

"Put the gun down, Miss Private Detective."

I laughed. "Not a chance. You'll cut her throat if I do."

"I'll cut her throat if you don't."

"Then I have nothing to lose. And neither does she."

He thought this over for a moment. "Keep your gun, then. It really doesn't matter."

"No, it doesn't. The cops will be here soon enough. All we have to do is wait."

He laughed, showing sharp white teeth. "Surely you can do better than that."

"Believe what you like," I told him. "But I found the girl you stuffed in the trunk. Police and ambulance are on their way."

"Then we'll have only a few minutes together, the three of us. Won't we?" he said gaily. "Never mind. It's time enough."

I looked at his knife hand and tried to make some calculations. To cut Eliane's throat he would need to move the knife. Right now he held it directly under her chin. Being right-handed, he would need to move the knife down and to the left. The question in my mind was one of physics—which would be faster, his hand or my bullet? I was willing to bet on my bullet. But could I hit him? The only parts of him that were visible were the arm that held Eliane, his shoulder, and the right side of his head. It would have to be his head. I sighted down the barrel of my .357, choosing his right eye as my target. Yeah. I could hit him. If he didn't move. If I didn't have one of my fugue attacks. If I didn't think about the fact that Eliane's head was so close to his.

Again, he anticipated me. Ducking behind Eliane, he taunted me. "Now you see me, now you don't. Go ahead. Shoot."

I ignored him.

"Oh, do come on," he urged impatiently. "If you think any one of us is going to walk out of here, you're wrong, wrong, wrong." His hand inside

Eliane's shirt did something violent and a sob burst from her throat. I ignored that, too. But the seconds ticked by and nothing changed. I realized with a clench of dismay that I'd have to change things. I needed an edge and only I could make it happen.

"Fell, listen to me. You could walk out of here," I told him. "Right now. I'd let you."

Silence. Then he said, "We both know you wouldn't do that. But for the sake of prolonging our little drama, please continue."

A light went on in my mind. There it was — my edge! Like a cobra, one part of my brain pounced on it. But I needed to continue my dialogue with Fell. I needed time to use that edge.

"Hey, you could have Laura," I said softly. "The girl you've wanted since you were sixteen. I know where she is. I'll tell you."

Did the hand holding the knife to Eliane's throat falter just a little? Would his sick fascination with Laura be enough to make him take the bait?

"Ah, but I'd have to give you this *psychologist,*" he said. "Dr. St. Cyr, who thought she'd get inside my head. I have business with her, too. Or maybe you don't know about that."

"Yeah, I know it. But think about things a minute. What you're going to do to Dr. St. Cyr will be over in an instant." I knew I was taking a terrible chance, but I had him talking, I had him halfway reeled in, and I wasn't going to quit. "One fountain of red and then nothing. Then I shoot you. You won't have time to savor it. Hell, you won't even see it." I dropped my voice. "But Laura, now that could be different. I know what you want to do to her, Martin. I know what those photos are all about. I know that you want to tie her up. To put your hands on her. To feel her. To smell her. I know that you need time. I could give you that time."

Silence.

I sang my siren song. "All the time you want. Think about it."

I saw Eliane swallow and realized she couldn't tolerate much more of this. How had she held on this long without breaking?

"You want the psychologist," he said in a flat voice.

Something inside me wound me tighter. *He's not buying it. He's not going to take the bait. He's going to kill her, dammit!*

"All right. I'll do it. Make the exchange. You can have her." He moved his hand from inside Eliane's shirt to her right shoulder and I saw with horrible clarity what he meant to do. He needed a brace, something to steady her while he cut her throat.

I called:

" 'Thou most lying slave,
Whom stripes may move, not kindness!' "

I cocked the .357's hammer, aiming at a spot just to the right of Eliane's ear.

Fell's hand froze.

I continued, my voice booming in what I hoped was the tone the magician Prospero might have used with Caliban, his monstrous servant. Caliban, whose part in *The Tempest* Fell had played that year when he was sixteen. Caliban, whom he had fancied himself to be. Tormented Caliban, "wound round with adders."

" 'Abhorred slave,
Which any print of goodness will not take,
Being capable of all ill!' "

I heard a delighted laugh. Fell responded:

" 'You taught me language; and my profit on't
Is, I know how to curse. The red plague rid you
For learning me your language.' "

I heard a sound which might have been a sob and he looked out from behind the safety of Eliane's head. "Here's my special red plague for you, *detective,*" he said, his face alight with glee, his knife hand descending.

I pulled the trigger.

The big gun *boomed* in the small cabin and through my weapon's sights, I saw both Fell and Eliane fall to the floor, tangled together. I shouted in horror, in denial, as I ran across the cabin and fell to my knees beside them. They were both still, the pool of blood they lay in spreading like the red plague Fell had cursed me with. Now it was I who sobbed. Gun still in my hand, I pulled Fell's arms away from Eliane and turned her so I could see what he had done to her.

"Caitlin?" she said, holding her bound hands out to me.

Her beautiful hair was sticky with blood and I brushed it off her face. She was weeping, and I saw in amazement that her throat bore only the shallow cut Fell had made earlier. My bullet had been faster than his hand after all. As for Fell, he lay on his side in his own blood, the back of his head blown out. I noted with dispassion that my bullet had entered his head just above his right eye. I hadn't hit the target after all.

"Caitlin?" Eliane asked again and I pulled her to a sitting position, wrapping my arms around her. "That blast. I can't hear," she said. "Will I be . . . deaf?" She began to sob, great racking bursts of fear and pain and I held her tighter.

"No," I said, reassuring her. "Your hearing will come back. I'm having the same problem." I knew what she feared, though. A black, soundless nowhere, a place more dreary than Caliban's cell, a prison to which Martin Fell had condemned her. "No. You won't be deaf."

I put my .357 back in its holster, found my knife, and cut Eliane free. I took her hands in mine, bent my head, and kissed her palms. She put her hands in my hair and pulled my head to her breasts. I put my arms around her. I felt her lay her head against mine. I heard the steady beat of her heart, the sigh of her breath. In the distance I heard sirens and, a few minutes later, the sound of heavy feet running up the makeshift stairway at the side of the *Sea Queen.*

SATURDAY

Chapter 14

The cool mathematical precision of Bach's music would normally have soothed my soul. Chaos defeated. Order restored. God's in her heaven and all's right with the world. But today the magic just wasn't there for me.

I sat in the audience at the Royal Victoria Conservatory of Music and watched eleven-year-old Jory take her piano exam. Lester sat on one side of me, Gray Ng on the other. Laura and Liz would do what they would. And I had made it. Against all odds, I was here. No one would be disappointed. No one's heart would be broken.

As far as I could tell, Jory played brilliantly. But my mind was not on her playing or indeed, on music at all. Instead of the dim, cavernous recital hall of the Conservatory, I saw instead the driveway of Eliane's house, from which I had just come.

It wasn't until well after midnight that officialdom in the person of the Sooke police was satisfied. I had called Sandy to send a constable to return the blubbering Theo to Oak Bay where, despite my promise to his mother, I intended to charge him with assault. It seems he hadn't run very far — the Sooke police had found him half-hidden behind one of the trawler's lifeboats. In the wee hours of the morning I had driven to the hospital to check on Romany, and I sat outside her room, waiting for her to feel like answering some questions. I had sent the distraught Lester home in a cab, where I fervently hoped he was having grave doubts about ever assisting me with another case.

A stern-looking nurse came out of Romany's room and closed the door behind her. "Just a few minutes," she said. I nodded.

Inside, Romany was bright-eyed and indignant. Finally, when she realized nothing dire was likely to happen, she confessed.

"It was the fax," she said sullenly. "The one that came for you from that Francis person. Eliane had me read it to her and when she found out that Theo Blalock was on the *Sea Queen* and that it was in drydock at that marina, she made me drive her there. She thought he was Martin Fell."

"What in hell did she plan to do?" I asked angrily. "Did she have a plan?"

"She just wanted to talk to him, you know, to Martin Fell. To ask him why he did that awful thing to her all those years ago. That was all. But she never got a chance to. They heard us drive up that little road behind the trawler and came to meet us. They didn't have to *hit* me," Romany huffed. "Listen, can you get me out of here? This gown is pretty embarrassing."

"Nothing doing. You stay there until the doctors let you go. Head wounds are nothing to mess around with." I winced, recalling mine.

"What about Eliane?"

"Her doctor says she'll be all right. The cut on her throat is superficial. The ringing in her ears is to be expected. She's probably ready to go. I'll drive her home."

"Did you call my mother? Agathe?"

"I called Agathe."

She subsided. "Okay."

I patted her hand. "See you later."

Eliane was waiting for me in her room, wearing a ridiculous lime green sweatshirt someone had kindly found for her, her hair loosely tied behind her head, a six-inch white bandage on her throat. I closed the door softly.

"Who's there?" she asked.

I felt that I had been punched under the heart. Her face, her voice, her *presence.* God, when would I get over this? I swallowed. "Caitlin."

She smiled and stood up.

"How do you feel?" I asked her.
"Alive."
"Do your ears ring?"
"A little."
"Mine, too. It'll pass."
"Have you come to take me home?"
"If you like."
"I'd like that very much," she said. "Can we go now? Or is there something else to be done?"
"No. As far as I know, we can just . . . leave. My car's outside." I crossed the room and took her hand, tucking her arm under mine as she had done in her library that afternoon days ago. We navigated halls and elevators, and then we stood in the parking lot. I opened my MG's passenger side door and guided her into her seat, conscious of every time I touched her. I had somehow thought that once this business with Martin Fell was concluded, her attraction for me would be over, too. Well, I was wrong.
I started the MG's engine and drove out of the hospital parking lot and onto the highway.
"What time is it?" she asked.
"About nine."
"It's going to be a nice day, isn't it?"
"Yeah. Blue sky, no clouds. Spring at last."
"Is there a pretty spot where we can stop?"
"Sure," I said, puzzled. "Let me find one." Up ahead a little gravel road led to a deserted, rocky beach. I slowed down and pulled over and we bounced down the narrow road to the water.
"Can you describe it to me?"
"Well, we're parked at the edge of a beach. It's

crescent-shaped. About fifty feet long. Big rocks up near the road, smaller rocks and pebbles down by the water. A little sand, too. Some pieces of driftwood here and there on the beach. The tide's going out. There are, oh, maybe half a dozen sandpipers down near the water." I looked out to sea. "The water's indigo. The sky's that soft powder blue you only see in the north."

"I want to see it," she said. She turned to face me in the car. "I decided last night that I'll go to Switzerland."

My heart sank. *Don't be a jerk,* I told myself. She ought to go. "For the eye surgery you were telling me about?"

"Yes. I've been putting the decision off. Finding reasons to delay. The chances of success are . . . good enough. I won't delay any longer."

"Good," I told her, feeling absurdly bereft. "When will you leave?"

"As soon as Romany's able to travel. A few weeks at most."

"Well . . . good," I said again.

"I want to see you."

It was suddenly very difficult to breathe. "Eliane, I—"

"Don't say anything," she said, and I realized she was crying. "I *will* see you," she told me, her voice husky. "And then, there are things we will talk about. But for now, take me home. Please."

We drove the rest of the way back to her house in silence. I honked as I drove up. Agathe opened the door and came hurrying down the steps.

Eliane opened the car door and swung her legs

out. "I will be back in September," she said. Then she half-turned back to me. She was, I saw, still crying. *"Au revoir."*

Agathe took her arm and led her toward the house. I watched her walk away. Then, because I wanted to say something, to conclude somehow, I bent and called, "Goodbye, Eliane," through the open car window. I thought she turned and said something, but I'm not sure because I'd gotten a bit of dust or pollen or something in my eyes. I watched her walk all the way to the big front door and when it closed behind her, I drove away.

"Bach *does* send you into la-la land, doesn't he?" whispered Tonia as she slid into a seat behind me. "I got your note and thought I'd join the festivities."

I gave a start. "Good," I whispered. "How was the conference?"

"Boring. I'm glad to be back. You can tell me all about the case at supper."

Lester showed the whites of his eyes like a spooked horse. Clearly he hoped the account I gave would be edited a little to omit his hysteria on the *Instead.* As for me, I had some editing to do, too. But try as I might, I couldn't feel guilty about Eliane. Tonia and I were . . . Tonia and I. We were the present tense; Eliane and I were the future conditional.

"Sure," I said, "I'll tell you all about it."

Lester cleared his throat.

I poked him with my elbow.

We surrendered ourselves once again to the music

and this time I let it take hold of my spirit. Maybe there really was joy and love and light and certitude and peace and help for pain. All those things that dour old Matthew Arnold asserted did not exist. Bach would disagree with him, I thought, listening to the measured, perfect cadences, the musical fiction of a predictable, knowable, comfortable universe.

I closed my eyes and, for the moment, believed.

A few of the publications of

THE NAIAD PRESS, INC.
P.O. Box 10543 • Tallahassee, Florida 32302
Phone (904) 539-5965
Toll-Free Order Number: 1-800-533-1973
Mail orders welcome. Please include 15% postage.

NIGHT SONGS by Penny Mickelbury. 224 pp. A Gianna Maglione Mystery. Second in a series.	ISBN 1-56280-097-3	$10.95
PAINTED MOON by Karin Kallmaker. 224 pp. Delicious Kallmaker romance.	ISBN 1-56280-075-2	9.95
THE MYSTERIOUS NAIAD edited by Katherine V. Forrest & Barbara Grier. 320 pp. Love stories by Naiad Press authors.	ISBN 1-56280-074-4	14.95
DAUGHTERS OF A CORAL DAWN by Katherine V. Forrest. 240 pp. Tenth Anniversay Edition.	ISBN 1-56280-104-X	10.95
BODY GUARD by Claire McNab. 208 pp. A Carol Ashton Mystery. 6th in a series.	ISBN 1-56280-073-6	9.95
CACTUS LOVE by Lee Lynch. 192 pp. Stories by the beloved storyteller.	ISBN 1-56280-071-X	9.95
SECOND GUESS by Rose Beecham. 216 pp. An Amanda Valentine Mystery. 2nd in a series.	ISBN 1-56280-069-8	9.95
THE SURE THING by Melissa Hartman. 208 pp. L.A. earthquake romance.	ISBN 1-56280-078-7	9.95
A RAGE OF MAIDENS by Lauren Wright Douglas. 240 pp. A Caitlin Reece Mystery. 6th in a series.	ISBN 1-56280-068-X	9.95
TRIPLE EXPOSURE by Jackie Calhoun. 224 pp. Romantic drama involving many characters.	ISBN 1-56280-067-1	9.95
UP, UP AND AWAY by Catherine Ennis. 192 pp. Delightful romance.	ISBN 1-56280-065-5	9.95
PERSONAL ADS by Robbi Sommers. 176 pp. Sizzling short stories.	ISBN 1-56280-059-0	9.95
FLASHPOINT by Katherine V. Forrest. 256 pp. Lesbian blockbuster!	ISBN 1-56280-043-4	22.95
CROSSWORDS by Penny Sumner. 256 pp. 2nd Victoria Cross Mystery.	ISBN 1-56280-064-7	9.95
SWEET CHERRY WINE by Carol Schmidt. 224 pp. A novel of suspense.	ISBN 1-56280-063-9	9.95

CERTAIN SMILES by Dorothy Tell. 160 pp. Erotic short stories.	ISBN 1-56280-066-3	9.95
EDITED OUT by Lisa Haddock. 224 pp. 1st Carmen Ramirez Mystery.	ISBN 1-56280-077-9	9.95
WEDNESDAY NIGHTS by Camarin Grae. 288 pp. Sexy adventure.	ISBN 1-56280-060-4	10.95
SMOKEY O by Celia Cohen. 176 pp. Relationships on the playing field.	ISBN 1-56280-057-4	9.95
KATHLEEN O'DONALD by Penny Hayes. 256 pp. Rose and Kathleen find each other and employment in 1909 NYC.	ISBN 1-56280-070-1	9.95
STAYING HOME by Elisabeth Nonas. 256 pp. Molly and Alix want a baby . . . or do they?	ISBN 1-56280-076-0	10.95
TRUE LOVE by Jennifer Fulton. 240 pp. Six lesbians searching for love in all the "right" places.	ISBN 1-56280-035-3	9.95
GARDENIAS WHERE THERE ARE NONE by Molleen Zanger. 176 pp. Why is Melanie inextricably drawn to the old house?	ISBN 1-56280-056-6	9.95
KEEPING SECRETS by Penny Mickelbury. 208 pp. A Gianna Maglione Mystery. First in a series.	ISBN 1-56280-052-3	9.95
THE ROMANTIC NAIAD edited by Katherine V. Forrest & Barbara Grier. 336 pp. Love stories by Naiad Press authors.	ISBN 1-56280-054-X	14.95
UNDER MY SKIN by Jaye Maiman. 336 pp. A Robin Miller mystery. 3rd in a series.	ISBN 1-56280-049-3.	10.95
STAY TOONED by Rhonda Dicksion. 144 pp. Cartoons — 1st collection since *Lesbian Survival Manual.*	ISBN 1-56280-045-0	9.95
CAR POOL by Karin Kallmaker. 272pp. Lesbians on wheels and then some!	ISBN 1-56280-048-5	9.95
NOT TELLING MOTHER: STORIES FROM A LIFE by Diane Salvatore. 176 pp. Her 3rd novel.	ISBN 1-56280-044-2	9.95
GOBLIN MARKET by Lauren Wright Douglas. 240pp. A Caitlin Reece Mystery. 5th in a series.	ISBN 1-56280-047-7	10.95
LONG GOODBYES by Nikki Baker. 256 pp. A Virginia Kelly mystery. 3rd in a series.	ISBN 1-56280-042-6	9.95
FRIENDS AND LOVERS by Jackie Calhoun. 224 pp. Mid-western Lesbian lives and loves.	ISBN 1-56280-041-8	10.95
THE CAT CAME BACK by Hilary Mullins. 208 pp. Highly praised Lesbian novel.	ISBN 1-56280-040-X	9.95
BEHIND CLOSED DOORS by Robbi Sommers. 192 pp. Hot, erotic short stories.	ISBN 1-56280-039-6	9.95

CLAIRE OF THE MOON by Nicole Conn. 192 pp. See the movie — read the book! ISBN 1-56280-038-8 10.95

SILENT HEART by Claire McNab. 192 pp. Exotic Lesbian romance. ISBN 1-56280-036-1 10.95

HAPPY ENDINGS by Kate Brandt. 272 pp. Intimate conversations with Lesbian authors. ISBN 1-56280-050-7 10.95

THE SPY IN QUESTION by Amanda Kyle Williams. 256 pp. 4th Madison McGuire. ISBN 1-56280-037-X 9.95

SAVING GRACE by Jennifer Fulton. 240 pp. Adventure and romantic entanglement. ISBN 1-56280-051-5 9.95

THE YEAR SEVEN by Molleen Zanger. 208 pp. Women surviving in a new world. ISBN 1-56280-034-5 9.95

CURIOUS WINE by Katherine V. Forrest. 176 pp. Tenth Anniversary Edition. The most popular contemporary Lesbian love story. ISBN 1-56280-053-1 10.95

Audio Book (2 cassettes) ISBN 1-56280-105-8 16.95

CHAUTAUQUA by Catherine Ennis. 192 pp. Exciting, romantic adventure. ISBN 1-56280-032-9 9.95

A PROPER BURIAL by Pat Welch. 192 pp. A Helen Black mystery. 3rd in a series. ISBN 1-56280-033-7 9.95

SILVERLAKE HEAT: A Novel of Suspense by Carol Schmidt. 240 pp. Rhonda is as hot as Laney's dreams. ISBN 1-56280-031-0 9.95

LOVE, ZENA BETH by Diane Salvatore. 224 pp. The most talked about lesbian novel of the nineties! ISBN 1-56280-030-2 10.95

A DOORYARD FULL OF FLOWERS by Isabel Miller. 160 pp. Stories incl. 2 sequels to *Patience and Sarah.* ISBN 1-56280-029-9 9.95

MURDER BY TRADITION by Katherine V. Forrest. 288 pp. A Kate Delafield Mystery. 4th in a series. ISBN 1-56280-002-7 9.95

THE EROTIC NAIAD edited by Katherine V. Forrest & Barbara Grier. 224 pp. Love stories by Naiad Press authors. ISBN 1-56280-026-4 13.95

DEAD CERTAIN by Claire McNab. 224 pp. A Carol Ashton mystery. 5th in a series. ISBN 1-56280-027-2 9.95

CRAZY FOR LOVING by Jaye Maiman. 320 pp. A Robin Miller mystery. 2nd in a series. ISBN 1-56280-025-6 9.95

STONEHURST by Barbara Johnson. 176 pp. Passionate regency romance. ISBN 1-56280-024-8 9.95

INTRODUCING AMANDA VALENTINE by Rose Beecham. 256 pp. An Amanda Valentine Mystery. First in a series. ISBN 1-56280-021-3 9.95

UNCERTAIN COMPANIONS by Robbi Sommers. 204 pp. Steamy, erotic novel. ISBN 1-56280-017-5 9.95

A TIGER'S HEART by Lauren W. Douglas. 240 pp. A Caitlin Reece mystery. 4th in a series.	ISBN 1-56280-018-3	9.95
PAPERBACK ROMANCE by Karin Kallmaker. 256 pp. A delicious romance.	ISBN 1-56280-019-1	9.95
MORTON RIVER VALLEY by Lee Lynch. 304 pp. Lee Lynch at her best!	ISBN 1-56280-016-7	9.95
THE LAVENDER HOUSE MURDER by Nikki Baker. 224 pp. A Virginia Kelly Mystery. 2nd in a series.	ISBN 1-56280-012-4	9.95
PASSION BAY by Jennifer Fulton. 224 pp. Passionate romance, virgin beaches, tropical skies.	ISBN 1-56280-028-0	10.95
STICKS AND STONES by Jackie Calhoun. 208 pp. Contemporary lesbian lives and loves.	ISBN 1-56280-020-5	9.95
DELIA IRONFOOT by Jeane Harris. 192 pp. Adventure for Delia and Beth in the Utah mountains.	ISBN 1-56280-014-0	9.95
UNDER THE SOUTHERN CROSS by Claire McNab. 192 pp. Romantic nights Down Under.	ISBN 1-56280-011-6	9.95
GRASSY FLATS by Penny Hayes. 256 pp. Lesbian romance in the '30s.	ISBN 1-56280-010-8	9.95
A SINGULAR SPY by Amanda K. Williams. 192 pp. 3rd Madison McGuire.	ISBN 1-56280-008-6	8.95
THE END OF APRIL by Penny Sumner. 240 pp. A Victoria Cross mystery. First in a series.	ISBN 1-56280-007-8	8.95
HOUSTON TOWN by Deborah Powell. 208 pp. A Hollis Carpenter mystery.	ISBN 1-56280-006-X	8.95
KISS AND TELL by Robbi Sommers. 192 pp. Scorching stories by the author of *Pleasures.*	ISBN 1-56280-005-1	10.95
STILL WATERS by Pat Welch. 208 pp. A Helen Black mystery. 2nd in a series.	ISBN 0-941483-97-5	9.95
TO LOVE AGAIN by Evelyn Kennedy. 208 pp. Wildly romantic love story.	ISBN 0-941483-85-1	9.95
IN THE GAME by Nikki Baker. 192 pp. A Virginia Kelly mystery. First in a series.	ISBN 1-56280-004-3	9.95
AVALON by Mary Jane Jones. 256 pp. A Lesbian Arthurian romance.	ISBN 0-941483-96-7	9.95
STRANDED by Camarin Grae. 320 pp. Entertaining, riveting adventure.	ISBN 0-941483-99-1	9.95
THE DAUGHTERS OF ARTEMIS by Lauren Wright Douglas. 240 pp. A Caitlin Reece mystery. 3rd in a series.	ISBN 0-941483-95-9	9.95
CLEARWATER by Catherine Ennis. 176 pp. Romantic secrets of a small Louisiana town.	ISBN 0-941483-65-7	8.95

THE HALLELUJAH MURDERS by Dorothy Tell. 176 pp. A Poppy Dillworth mystery. 2nd in a series. ISBN 0-941483-88-6 8.95

SECOND CHANCE by Jackie Calhoun. 256 pp. Contemporary Lesbian lives and loves. ISBN 0-941483-93-2 9.95

BENEDICTION by Diane Salvatore. 272 pp. Striking, contemporary romantic novel. ISBN 0-941483-90-8 9.95

BLACK IRIS by Jeane Harris. 192 pp. Caroline's hidden past . . . ISBN 0-941483-68-1 8.95

TOUCHWOOD by Karin Kallmaker. 240 pp. Loving, May/December romance. ISBN 0-941483-76-2 9.95

COP OUT by Claire McNab. 208 pp. A Carol Ashton mystery. 4th in a series. ISBN 0-941483-84-3 9.95

THE BEVERLY MALIBU by Katherine V. Forrest. 288 pp. A Kate Delafield Mystery. 3rd in a series. ISBN 0-941483-48-7 10.95

THAT OLD STUDEBAKER by Lee Lynch. 272 pp. Andy's affair with Regina and her attachment to her beloved car. ISBN 0-941483-82-7 9.95

PASSION'S LEGACY by Lori Paige. 224 pp. Sarah is swept into the arms of Augusta Pym in this delightful historical romance. ISBN 0-941483-81-9 8.95

THE PROVIDENCE FILE by Amanda Kyle Williams. 256 pp. Second Madison McGuire ISBN 0-941483-92-4 8.95

I LEFT MY HEART by Jaye Maiman. 320 pp. A Robin Miller Mystery. First in a series. ISBN 0-941483-72-X 9.95

THE PRICE OF SALT by Patricia Highsmith (writing as Claire Morgan). 288 pp. Classic lesbian novel, first issued in 1952 . . . acknowledged by its author under her own, very famous, name. ISBN 1-56280-003-5 9.95

SIDE BY SIDE by Isabel Miller. 256 pp. From beloved author of *Patience and Sarah.* ISBN 0-941483-77-0 9.95

STAYING POWER: LONG TERM LESBIAN COUPLES by Susan E. Johnson. 352 pp. Joys of coupledom. ISBN 0-941-483-75-4 14.95

SLICK by Camarin Grae. 304 pp. Exotic, erotic adventure. ISBN 0-941483-74-6 9.95

NINTH LIFE by Lauren Wright Douglas. 256 pp. A Caitlin Reece mystery. 2nd in a series. ISBN 0-941483-50-9 8.95

PLAYERS by Robbi Sommers. 192 pp. Sizzling, erotic novel. ISBN 0-941483-73-8 9.95

MURDER AT RED ROOK RANCH by Dorothy Tell. 224 pp. A Poppy Dillworth mystery. 1st in a series. ISBN 0-941483-80-0 8.95

LESBIAN SURVIVAL MANUAL by Rhonda Dicksion. 112 pp. Cartoons! ISBN 0-941483-71-1 8.95

A ROOM FULL OF WOMEN by Elisabeth Nonas. 256 pp. Contemporary Lesbian lives. ISBN 0-941483-69-X 9.95

THEME FOR DIVERSE INSTRUMENTS by Jane Rule. 208 pp. Powerful romantic lesbian stories. ISBN 0-941483-63-0 8.95

CLUB 12 by Amanda Kyle Williams. 288 pp. Espionage thriller featuring a lesbian agent! ISBN 0-941483-64-9 8.95

DEATH DOWN UNDER by Claire McNab. 240 pp. A Carol Ashton mystery. 3rd in a series. ISBN 0-941483-39-8 9.95

MONTANA FEATHERS by Penny Hayes. 256 pp. Vivian and Elizabeth find love in frontier Montana. ISBN 0-941483-61-4 8.95

LIFESTYLES by Jackie Calhoun. 224 pp. Contemporary Lesbian lives and loves. ISBN 0-941483-57-6 9.95

WILDERNESS TREK by Dorothy Tell. 192 pp. Six women on vacation learning "new" skills. ISBN 0-941483-60-6 8.95

MURDER BY THE BOOK by Pat Welch. 256 pp. A Helen Black Mystery. First in a series. ISBN 0-941483-59-2 9.95

THERE'S SOMETHING I'VE BEEN MEANING TO TELL YOU Ed. by Loralee MacPike. 288 pp. Gay men and lesbians coming out to their children. ISBN 0-941483-44-4 9.95

LIFTING BELLY by Gertrude Stein. Ed. by Rebecca Mark. 104 pp. Erotic poetry. ISBN 0-941483-51-7 8.95

AFTER THE FIRE by Jane Rule. 256 pp. Warm, human novel by this incomparable author. ISBN 0-941483-45-2 8.95

THREE WOMEN by March Hastings. 232 pp. Golden oldie. A triangle among wealthy sophisticates. ISBN 0-941483-43-6 8.95

PLEASURES by Robbi Sommers. 204 pp. Unprecedented eroticism. ISBN 0-941483-49-5 8.95

EDGEWISE by Camarin Grae. 372 pp. Spellbinding adventure. ISBN 0-941483-19-3 9.95

FATAL REUNION by Claire McNab. 224 pp. A Carol Ashton mystery. 2nd in a series. ISBN 0-941483-40-1 8.95

IN EVERY PORT by Karin Kallmaker. 228 pp. Jessica's sexy, adventuresome travels. ISBN 0-941483-37-7 9.95

OF LOVE AND GLORY by Evelyn Kennedy. 192 pp. Exciting WWII romance. ISBN 0-941483-32-0 8.95

CLICKING STONES by Nancy Tyler Glenn. 288 pp. Love transcending time. ISBN 0-941483-31-2 9.95

SOUTH OF THE LINE by Catherine Ennis. 216 pp. Civil War adventure. ISBN 0-941483-29-0 8.95

WOMAN PLUS WOMAN by Dolores Klaich. 300 pp. Supurb Lesbian overview. ISBN 0-941483-28-2 9.95

THE FINER GRAIN by Denise Ohio. 216 pp. Brilliant young college lesbian novel. ISBN 0-941483-11-8 8.95

OCTOBER OBSESSION by Meredith More. Josie's rich, secret Lesbian life. ISBN 0-941483-18-5 8.95

BEFORE STONEWALL: THE MAKING OF A GAY AND LESBIAN COMMUNITY by Andrea Weiss & Greta Schiller. 96 pp., 25 illus. ISBN 0-941483-20-7 7.95

OSTEN'S BAY by Zenobia N. Vole. 204 pp. Sizzling adventure romance set on Bonaire. ISBN 0-941483-15-0 8.95

LESSONS IN MURDER by Claire McNab. 216 pp. A Carol Ashton mystery. First in a series. ISBN 0-941483-14-2 9.95

YELLOWTHROAT by Penny Hayes. 240 pp. Margarita, bandit, kidnaps Julia. ISBN 0-941483-10-X 8.95

SAPPHISTRY: THE BOOK OF LESBIAN SEXUALITY by Pat Califia. 3d edition, revised. 208 pp. ISBN 0-941483-24-X 10.95

CHERISHED LOVE by Evelyn Kennedy. 192 pp. Erotic Lesbian love story. ISBN 0-941483-08-8 9.95

THE SECRET IN THE BIRD by Camarin Grae. 312 pp. Striking, psychological suspense novel. ISBN 0-941483-05-3 8.95

TO THE LIGHTNING by Catherine Ennis. 208 pp. Romantic Lesbian 'Robinson Crusoe' adventure. ISBN 0-941483-06-1 8.95

DREAMS AND SWORDS by Katherine V. Forrest. 192 pp. Romantic, erotic, imaginative stories. ISBN 0-941483-03-7 8.95

MEMORY BOARD by Jane Rule. 336 pp. Memorable novel about an aging Lesbian couple. ISBN 0-941483-02-9 10.95

THE ALWAYS ANONYMOUS BEAST by Lauren Wright Douglas. 224 pp. A Caitlin Reece mystery. First in a series. ISBN 0-941483-04-5 8.95

PARENTS MATTER by Ann Muller. 240 pp. Parents' relationships with Lesbian daughters and gay sons. ISBN 0-930044-91-6 9.95

THE BLACK AND WHITE OF IT by Ann Allen Shockley. 144 pp. Short stories. ISBN 0-930044-96-7 7.95

SAY JESUS AND COME TO ME by Ann Allen Shockley. 288 pp. Contemporary romance. ISBN 0-930044-98-3 8.95

MURDER AT THE NIGHTWOOD BAR by Katherine V. Forrest. 240 pp. A Kate Delafield mystery. Second in a series. ISBN 0-930044-92-4 10.95

WINGED DANCER by Camarin Grae. 228 pp. Erotic Lesbian adventure story. ISBN 0-930044-88-6 8.95

PAZ by Camarin Grae. 336 pp. Romantic Lesbian adventurer with the power to change the world. ISBN 0-930044-89-4 8.95

SOUL SNATCHER by Camarin Grae. 224 pp. A puzzle, an adventure, a mystery — Lesbian romance. ISBN 0-930044-90-8 8.95

THE LOVE OF GOOD WOMEN by Isabel Miller. 224 pp. Long-awaited new novel by the author of the beloved *Patience and Sarah.* ISBN 0-930044-81-9 8.95

THE HOUSE AT PELHAM FALLS by Brenda Weathers. 240 pp. Suspenseful Lesbian ghost story. ISBN 0-930044-79-7 7.95

HOME IN YOUR HANDS by Lee Lynch. 240 pp. More stories from the author of *Old Dyke Tales.* ISBN 0-930044-80-0 7.95

PEMBROKE PARK by Michelle Martin. 256 pp. Derring-do and daring romance in Regency England. ISBN 0-930044-77-0 7.95

THE LONG TRAIL by Penny Hayes. 248 pp. Vivid adventures of two women in love in the old west. ISBN 0-930044-76-2 8.95

AN EMERGENCE OF GREEN by Katherine V. Forrest. 288 pp. Powerful novel of sexual discovery. ISBN 0-930044-69-X 9.95

THE LESBIAN PERIODICALS INDEX edited by Claire Potter. 432 pp. Author & subject index. ISBN 0-930044-74-6 12.95

DESERT OF THE HEART by Jane Rule. 224 pp. A classic; basis for the movie *Desert Hearts.* ISBN 0-930044-73-8 10.95

TORCHLIGHT TO VALHALLA by Gale Wilhelm. 128 pp. Classic novel by a great Lesbian writer. ISBN 0-930044-68-1 7.95

LESBIAN NUNS: BREAKING SILENCE edited by Rosemary Curb and Nancy Manahan. 432 pp. Unprecedented autobiographies of religious life. ISBN 0-930044-62-2 9.95

THE SWASHBUCKLER by Lee Lynch. 288 pp. Colorful novel set in Greenwich Village in the sixties. ISBN 0-930044-66-5 8.95

SEX VARIANT WOMEN IN LITERATURE by Jeannette Howard Foster. 448 pp. Literary history. ISBN 0-930044-65-7 8.95

A HOT-EYED MODERATE by Jane Rule. 252 pp. Hard-hitting essays on gay life; writing; art. ISBN 0-930044-57-6 7.95

AMATEUR CITY by Katherine V. Forrest. 224 pp. A Kate Delafield mystery. First in a series. ISBN 0-930044-55-X 10.95

THE SOPHIE HOROWITZ STORY by Sarah Schulman. 176 pp. Engaging novel of madcap intrigue. ISBN 0-930044-54-1 7.95

THE YOUNG IN ONE ANOTHER'S ARMS by Jane Rule. 224 pp. Classic Jane Rule. ISBN 0-930044-53-3 9.95

OLD DYKE TALES by Lee Lynch. 224 pp. Extraordinary stories of our diverse Lesbian lives. ISBN 0-930044-51-7 8.95

AGAINST THE SEASON by Jane Rule. 224 pp. Luminous, complex novel of interrelationships. ISBN 0-930044-48-7 8.95

LOVERS IN THE PRESENT AFTERNOON by Kathleen Fleming. 288 pp. A novel about recovery and growth. ISBN 0-930044-46-0 8.95